You 

Los Angeles, California

ISBN: 978-0692869703

Book design by Kelli Evans

Cover design by Michael Harris

www.DemetriusHarris.com

Printed in the United States of America

THIS IS KNOT WHAT I PRAYED FOR

Publishers Notice:

This book is a work of fiction. Names, characters, places, and incidents were created by the author and his imagination and is used fictitiously. Any resemblance to actual persons, dead or alive, business establishments, brands, events, or locations is entirely coincidental.

D.E. Harris

THIS IS KNOT WHAT I PRAYED FOR

A former manager for Gannett Indianapolis Star, D. E. Harris' literary content has been published through a trio of books and an array of columns for major magazines across the U.S. When not creating plots and developing scenes, the wordsmith relishes moments with family and loved ones, and takes delight in movies and comedy shows.

Acknowledgements

Thanks:

To The Most High, who constantly pours strength into me.

To my Mom, for showing me a love like no other.

To my Dad, for endless moral support.

To my companion, for constantly putting up with me and persistent help towards my vision.

To grandfather Crowley, for sharing with me your wisdom.

To my late grandmother, Rosie Crowley, I think about you often. You are always in my heart. #CancerSucks

To The Harris grandparents, for spiritual counsel through how you live your lives.

To my siblings, for being the best in the world.

To my aunts and uncles, Cathy/Michael, Traci/Marcus, Corey/Stacie, Cheryl, George, Kenneth, and a host of others. You all mean the world to me.

To my cousins, Jelani, Lamont, Jamal, Lauren, Chelsea, Kristina, Desiree, CJ, Cori, and Cierra, don't stop encouraging me.

To my nieces and nephews, Maleena, Donovon, Tre, Mariah, Mikey, and Michaela, and little Ceej, never stop dreaming.

To my creative team, Kelli, Rhonda, Mikey, and Corey for

your input and opinions.

To Charles, Nikki, and Rhonda, for being consistent in our friendship.

To my newest friends, Chad & Gabrielle (GabeBabeTV), JD. I'm glad of our connection through Kelli.

Special thanks to Pastor Ronnie and Pamela Evans, and the Grace Memorial Baptist church, for allowing me to incorporate my flowery imagination into the theatre ministry.

And special thanks to my high school English and Literature teacher, Crystal Murff. Our country needs more educators like you.

And to all my relatives by blood or marriage, and even friends, you've all played some role in who I am today.

Poem By: D. E. Harris

Give someone words today. Not just any words, but an army of word weaponry manufactured for warfare. Word devices fused to blow up desolate moods.

Give them a black belt in word art, techniques they can use for self-assurance against their attackers.

Give them a word aid kit; word ointments to clean their wounded spirits and a bandage of words to protect against dirty words along with scissors to cut away negative words.

And give them a warm word blanket because there are cold words out there, and a bottle of word biotics to soothe their pain.

Feed them a warm word meal; two compliments, a side of encouragement & motivation, and a sweet word for dessert.

And give them a lasting word to go, for life's daily combat. Because the truth of the matter is, EVERYONE is fighting a battle you know nothing about.

FORTHCOMING CONTENT

She was like a prized possession being showcased in a maroon strapless dress; a one-piece outer garment that told a story; a narrative of erotic events; shiny; zipped in the back; cleavage partially exposed; hugging her hips like a mother's love.

Twirling a strand of her hair, "what's six inches long, two inches wide, and drives women wild?"

He laughed away at her inquiry.

"There you go again," he said, a reverence to her bold overtures.

She smiled coyly; she was a super sexual, and wasn't into expressive symbols like roses and candy. She gave precedence to a simple bottle of wine or to fuck on hotel balconies.

"Ummm." he mumbled aloud, as he could discern she was preparing him a platform for something exotic. It was a war between her will versus his morals. And the way he gazed at her she already knew that he lost the battle.

She was a piece of work. Like a difficult puzzle. Conventional with an edginess to her. She was the kind of girl that expected a man to open the door for her, but dared him to slap her on the butt when she walked by.

All business matters were complete. The twosome dallied around the room on opposite ends of the futon, exchanging laughs, smiles, and butterfly babbles. Crossbreeding sips of wine with trifling topics, she began moving in ways designated to catch his eye; wanted him to know he had clearance for go-ahead maneuvers.

She stood up from the futon and strutted over to the short espresso table across the room; leaning over further than necessary. She was wearing a knee length summer dress and what she like to call her Betty Wright classic pumps; a musical artist, with a popular song titled *No Pain No Gain*. These were the kind of heels that ached her feet but was a sexy distraction.

Imani was finished writing down her reasons for why she loved him. She had a herd of them. Lamont was completely unlike any other person she encountered. He birthed her a spiritual life, acquainting her with the Jesus that lived in him; who saw her potential while in her predicament; treating her like a normal person but yet unconventionally; in manners unfamiliar to her conscience. In her secular life, normal was being born a crack baby. Normal was unshared emotions with her dope-fiend-prostitute mother. Normal was being molested by her uncle, cousin, and neighborhood mechanic. Normal was physical abuse by her grandmother who raised her not out of love but for financial gain. She was paid by the state. Normal was being hated by that same grandmother, because Imani's mother, had sex with grandma's boyfriend years ago. Normal for Imani was in and out of foster homes, all throughout childhood. She didn't graduate from high school. She ran away at 17, moved to Charlotte, North Carolina, and started stripping at Club Onyx, where married men, pimps and bachelors viewed her only in sexual conquest. That was normal for Imani. That's all she knew. Each of her experiences with men were sexual. They were sex demons and women were angelic sex slaves, at least from her perspective. So when she met Lamont she was drawn to him. He was fascinating. Winsome. Different; like a foreign country. That's why she calls him 'Kuntry'. He edified her. He was her first of many. The first to introduce her to his mom, who was the first to embrace her as a daughter. The first to tell her he was proud of her. The first to compliment her character. The first to invite her to church. The first to do her a goodwill favor. The first to touch her without actually touching her. And she was touched by it. She had a virgin blush. No carnal knowledge of a man that loved her unconditionally.

Chapter ONE

Thursday, April 25th, 6:34 P.M.

Walking into the master bedroom suite, "You almost ready?" he asked impatiently. She was staring into the mirror, carefully applying her eyeliner.

"Just about."

"Hurry up now because we are going to be late."

They had reservations for dinner at Sambuca Restaurant in downtown Nashville, Tennessee.

"Okay baby I think I'm ready now" she responded, immediately upon placing the pencil onto the granite counter top.

She was a Midwest Missy, from Indianapolis, Indiana. Brebeuf Jesuit graduate, but not your ordinary private school kind of girl. She was very outgoing, brimmed with humor, and relatively sassy.

She faced his direction as he was standing at the threshold of the door.

"So tell me baby, how do I look?" she asked. It was a routine question upon getting dressed. She always sought his approval.

Placing her hand onto her hip, she undertook an exaggerated disposition, broadcasting her diamond tennis bracelet. She was wearing a blue wrap dress, showcasing sexy features of her *Kamica Hampton* high heels; a distinctive stiletto with a unique ankle cuff closure flaunting a sumptuous bow with sateen finish. Coined as *The Wealth Style*.

He stared at her, attentively, toying his chin hairs between his thumb and index finger as if he was dissecting scripture. He was a man of the cloth; Pastor of Abundant Life, one of the most recognized multi-cultural churches in Nashville.

Judging by the look on his face, she knew he wasn't content.

Cole exhaled a deep breath. "Ummm...something is not quite right" he said.

Jenna calculated his statement.

"Really?" she inquired, contorting her eyebrows. It was a delayed response.

"I mean, don't get me wrong. You look fantastic. But it seems like...like...like...I don't know...like something is missing or out of place."

"Well what is it babe?" she asked. She was impatient to know.

In a concerned tone, "Is it my hair?"

She was wearing sultry curls that took on a life of its own; a perfect balance between short and medium length. Just enough to work with but not too much that it feels weighed down. And the few loose tendrils dangling from the corner of her face were universally flattering.

"No, no, no. It's definitely not your hair. I'm feeling that hairstyle on you."

She turned towards the full-length mirror on the door of the walk-in closet.

"Well is it my dress...is it too tight...too lose?" she asked, focusing on her revolving physique.

"Nah, it is not the dress baby."

She proceeded in her self-inspection, conscious of every detail; adjusting her dress and voluptuous breasts. He watched her through the mirror for an indefinite number of seconds.

Damn, I shouldn't have never opened my big mouth he thought to himself.

He elevated his forearm, and glanced down at his faddish timekeeper.

Intensifying his voice, "Jenna it's time to go."

"Calm down Cole! Just give me a minute. You know I hate leaving the house not dressed up to par! ...You are the one that said I didn't look right."

He exhaled a breath of frustration.

"Boobie, I didn't say you don't look right, I just simply said that it seems like something is missing that's all."

"Exactly, and we can leave as soon as I figure it out...besides, I was kind of feeling that way as well," she stated, as she was still examining herself in the mirror.

Jenna turned around, facing him. Cole was now an arm's length away.

"Oh, I know what it is. I need some lipstick."

She reached for the drawer knob underneath the sink.

He grabbed her wrist, stopping her progress.

"No, no, no, baby, it's not the lipstick...I'm not sure what it is, but I know it's not the lipstick."

"What is it then Cole?" she asked. She was a bit unsettled.

"Stand back and let me take a closer look at you again."

She took a backwards step, and he began to visually size her up; quietly.

About a dozen seconds elapsed; she couldn't hold her peace.

"You want me to put on one of my necklaces?"

Nodding his head from side to side, "no honey, don't worry about that."

Extending her wrist towards him, "Okay. You think I should take off this bracelet and put on the watch you bought me last year?"

His eyes fastened on the bracelet; it was a prolonged observation.

She exhibited a smile, "yea I knew that was it! Wasn't it jellybean?" (His occasional pet name from her.)

She was elated, feeling assured by her own discernment of him. He was her confidant of three years.

"Yep I knew that was it. You have been complaining a lot lately about me wearing it...that's what it is...am I right jellybean...you want me to wear the watch...is that what you want?"

"I want you to marry me," he unwaveringly emitted, staring into her green eyes.

Unable to register his words, she appeared

quizzical, incomprehensible.

He lowered down to one knee.

Jenna was stunned, speechless, with an increased heartbeat, along with rapid breaths, as if she was hyperventilating. This was unexpected although she knew he was the one. But so did Cole; ever since that morning he first came into contact with her at the coffee shop on Melrose Street in Los Angeles. It was a chance encounter. Jenna was out there auditioning for a role in a film. Her sexy swagger caught his eye. And his friendly 'hello' quickly turned into a long conversation, followed by many to come.

He reached into his pocket and removed a sophisticated *Tiffany* Blue Box.

He exalted it, peeking up into her receptive eyes, and pulled back the lid.

It was a princess cut, four carat glaring diamond ring, isolated on white background.

"Boobie, this is what was missing. This ring, symbolizing my love for you."

"Please Jenna, make me an honest man," he humbly pleaded.

"Will you marry me?"

Thursday February 6th, 8:29 P.M.---Two Years Later

Sitting at the edge of the bed, "read my lips," she commanded in a seductive tone.

He channeled his eyes directly on them; shiny, textured with gloss, anticipating dirty talk.

Slowly, she swayed her head from left to right, expressing denial.

"Uhn-Uhn honey, my other lips."

She lodged backwards on the bed, pulling her sexy legs behind her head into a pretzel position. She was panty-less, only wearing a black long sleeve fishnet top, eager to gratify his visual senses.

"Look how wet and ready I am for you papi."

She was affectionately playing with her Brazilian waxed genitalia as he gazed intensely.

"Don't you want to put your dick in there?" she said, wildly alluring him through words and imagination.

"Yessssss..."

He had a sultry look, gently biting his lower lip.

"But..."

Mesmerized by her fondling the creases of her glistening geni lips, there were gaps in his verbiage.

"Not before I bury my face in your pussy...annnd...ummm."

He was momentarily lost for words.

"Penetrate your narrow slit with my tongue."

He moistened his lips, signaling his appetite.

At a slackened pace... "And with it, I will do figure eights, then the alphabet...in reverse, from Z to A, but I'll stop at letter J."

Rubbing her throbbing clitoris, "why would you stop?" she asked sensually.

"Because at letter J, you will be cumming down my chin."

She pursed her lips... "Ewww daddy, I like that."

"And I love that you like it," he replied, as he started to caress his manhood from the padded leather executive chair he normally sat in.

She rose to her knees, with her back facing him.

He couldn't help to notice her incredible bottom, with a Lion head tattoo on the left cheek, and *D' Ass* inked on the right cheek.

She leaned forward, dipping her lower back; ass elevated, face slightly above the mattress covered with soft, silky purple satin sheets.

Tantalizing him, she moved her ass unsteadily as he fetish the noise of her cheeks colliding together.

"Do you like what you see?" she asked, reassuringly.

"Oh yes, no doubt."

"Well prove it to me...stand up and let me see how hard that dick is you touching on" she demanded, surveying him through the large frame-less wall mirror above her headboard.

He stood up from the chair unashamedly exposing himself.

"Ohhh daddy you have convinced me."

There was an endless moment of silence while gazing at each other mysteriously. He was undeniably lust-struck by her powerful glance.

As the absence of speech continued, her eyes began to talk. He scanned deeply into them, attempting to interpret the visual messages.

"Go head, let me see you jerk on it" she petitioned, gripping her curvaceous bottom with both hands. Her sex appeal was intoxicating.

He started groping his upright disc at a moderate pace; groaning lightly; eyes fixed on her ass; he had an unreasoning fondness for it, just as nearly all men. It was her most desirable feature.

She spread apart her butt cheeks.

"So tell me big daddy...which hole do you want to fuck?" she solicited in a harsh tone. Naughty language came naturally for her; she had no boundaries.

Knock Knock Knock

Startled by the strikes at the office door, his heart was racing; quickly, he slammed shut the lid to his stylish laptop that was on his mahogany desk. It was a Stealth Macbook Pro, his most valued gadget. Not only did he use it for business purposes, but he conveniently logged onto *CherokeesFetishes.com* where as a member he was able to stimulate his sexual desires via live interaction over the web-cam.

"Just a second!" he said, while fastening his pants. He was panicky and apprehensive.

As soon as he opened the door, "hey Pastor" she said.

A former flight attendant, she gave up the friendly skies and relocated to Nashville after Cole extended her a position as the church administrator a year into their existence. The ministry rapidly blossomed and there was a need for someone to assume the role. Coupling the offer with the untimely death of her father, she wanted to get away and believed the move would be like a breath of fresh air.

"Sorry to interrupt you."

Expressing dissatisfaction, "Naomi you know goodness well you not disturbing me, and I know that you are aware of my open-door policy with our staff."

"Yea I know; I know...but that's just the way I am."

He exhaled a deep breath of sarcastic-frustration.

Naomi smirked.

"Anyways, here is a check for payment from Traci and Kevin; it's for their *Before-You-Say-I-Do* classes. She just dropped it off with me up front."

"Okie dokie," he said, after she handed him the check and trotted back to her work area.

Traci was one of his members, several months away from entering into a sacred union with Kevin Bridgewater. Pastor Cole was the officiating officer for the wedding ceremony.

After closing the door, he slumped down on the chair, covering his face with his hands. He felt relieved that he just avoided disaster.

Chapter TWO

Friday, February 7th...8:23 P.M.

It was a starlit evening as the affluent bombarded the Sirrah Bar, the most sophisticated lounge in Nashville. Graced with elegant, rich design features throughout the property, guests were captivated by the intimate décor details along with custom graphite colored ceramic floors throughout the building.

"Let me tell yall young ladies this."

She was a featured panelist, advanced in years, early 50's, and seemed to have accumulated knowledge and experience.

"Excuse my French but as a married woman, you ought to be the absolute biggest hoe your husband knows!" she firmly stated.

Instantly, there was a seditious roar of laughs and loud remarks by the audience as they were thunderstruck by her disdainful remark. And next to the bar was the moderator, who stood frozen, wide-eyed, with her mouth slightly open. Although her choice of words came unexpectedly, her input was very befitting.

The atmosphere tranquilized and her expression melted away... "Ohhhhhh-kaaaay now," she spoke into the mic, wearing her usual radiant smile. A vibrant, popular lifestyle vlogger from the United Kingdom, Zoella was able to draw out all emotional nuances from the crowd.

"Who else has a question for our panelists?" She asked. It was a wine tasting, but unconventional to normal customs; present was mass media personnel from Cosmopolitan, Oprah, and Glamour magazines, as well as FAWN (For All Women Network). Themed *IS A GOOD MAN REALLY HARD TO FIND*?, their senses were ravished by wine, comedy, poetry, and an openly raw panel discussion on love and relationships.

Noticing the woman's raised hand, she proceeded her direction and held the microphone near her face.

She was a few shades darker than the average Caucasian; curvy-petite, wearing an Egyptian skirt paired with a solid black top.

"My question is for Trent."

Founder of '*REHAB TIME*,' a Christian based non-profit organization; he was a prolific motivational speaker with over 200k twitter followers, whose counsel heavily influenced the thoughts and minds of many people.

All eyes transitioned towards her.

"My boyfriend, who's a black guy by the way...we have been seeing each other for about seven years...since our junior year of college. Besides the great deal of stares we get for being an interracial couple, we have our private battles from time to time, but for the most part, everything is fairly well with us and I love him and I know he really loves me. So my question is, why do you feel he has yet asked to marry me? Coming from a man, what is the delay?"

"Well let me ask you a question," Trent mentioned.

"Do you guys ever discuss marriage or have you told him what you want and expect to be married?"

"Oh yea! We've talked about it numerous of times and he knows that's what I really want. Not only that, I actually show him what I am about. I cook for him, I wash clothes, pack his lunch for work, I give him some very frequently (she couldn't resist a smile), I mean, I do it all...And I know that he knows I am a good person, but for whatever reason, he has not proposed to me. So I'm just confused about why he hasn't and what else you think I should do." she expressed in a defeated tone.

Exhaling a deep breath, he could sense her dissatisfaction.

"Well ma'am, your question is pretty common and I'm sure many women can relate to your predicament. That being said..."

He looked amongst the crowd as a whole.

"For every woman in this building, hear me out...It does not matter how good of a woman you are to a man...you can cook, clean, support, and do everything under the sun to prove to him your worth and value. Unfortunately, you will *never*, *ever*, *ever-ever*, be good enough..."

He paused for a quick second.

"If!... he is not ready."

"You can say that again!" someone blurted out from the overflowing occupants.

There was a round of applause by many, affirming their satisfaction of Trent's sentiments.

"Alright, alright," Zoella said, surveying the room of raised hands.

"It's time to get a question from a guy...we been hearing from you ladies pretty much the whole night."

"What's your name and who is your question for?"

He stood up from the stool he was sitting in adjacent to the bar; he was over six feet.

He retrieved the mic from Zoella's grasp.

"My name is Wyatt and my question is for Cole."

Appearing to be in his late 30's, he was fair-skinned; creamy blonde hair; with a nicely trimmed beard, and the pitch of his voice was baritone. The ladies were drawn to his masculinity.

"Just recently on New Year's Eve, a friend of mine had a get-together at his house and he had many of his friends and colleagues present....well anyway, I met this woman there that night, we randomly just started talking and just like shooting the breeze...and in a flash, I was captivated by her personality and sense of humor...she had such a warmness about her...so that whole evening we just talked and laughed and we exchanged numbers...and ever since that night, we have been hanging out frequently and spending time with one another...like we are really hitting it off..."

He simpered, breaking his verbalism.

"But point is, I don't want to speak too soon and I'm kind of unsure, which is why I am seeking your opinion...Now I know this may sound kind of crazy given it has only been a few weeks, but I'm honestly starting to feel like I love her."

"Awwwwwwe!" Zoella compassionately expressed aloud, smiling plenty.

With moderate joy, "how sweet!" another woman uttered.

There were continual utters of genuine *Awwwwes*, blended with a touch of sarcasm as they were persuaded by his eloquence.

He had an endearing grin.

"But anyway Cole, my question is, do you believe in love at first sight...is that possible?"

Reciting his question, "Do I believe in love at first sight."

"That's a good question Wyatt...and my answer to that is yes, it is possible...and I say that because back in Genesis, when God presented Eve to Adam, the bible declares that he was instantly ravished with joy when he said '*Bone of my bone, flesh of my flesh*'...he was elated to be in the presence of another human being, someone that was like-minded and similar looking to him...many theologians equate this feeling to love, which is why God allowed for them to become husband and wife...and also when he saw her, he wasn't looking at her sexually or lustfully, because sex had not yet been thought of or created. It wasn't until later on in scripture when God spoke sex into existence, telling them to be fruitful and multiply...and furthermore, it would have been a sin for him to look at her with a lustful heart, but as we know there was no such thing as sin at that present time...so yes based on those biblical facts I just gave you, love at first sight is possible..."

Modifying his voice, *"however."*

"Given that sex actually do exist in today's world and we know that beforehand, more times than not, many people confuse their lustful bliss with love...meaning, lust often times feels just like love, until it's time for a sacrifice."

There was an extensive clapping of the hands by the crowd, as they expressed their approval and appreciation for his insight.

"Okay. We are going to take one more question before we go to intermission" Zoella mentioned.

She noticed someone raising their hand in her peripheral vision. He was standing by the glass door leading to the open-air courtyard, centered alongside a conspicuous pool.

Making direct eye contact, Zoella was brightening in her face, smiling favorably; foretasting an empty-headed question.

She walked over to him; he was the headline comedian of the night; the one responsible for their stomachs aching from laughter earlier.

"Shang, what do you have to ask our panelist?"

A highly sought after comedian, he had appeared on Saturday Night Live, Comedy Central, and an array of cameos in movies and television shows.

"My question is..."

He had a serious disposition, but people were still

laughing within.

"How do you politely ask for some head?"

"Good question!" A random male shouted.

There was an outburst of explosive chuckles throughout the room, but it wasn't long before the commotion ceased.

"Oh that's simple. I can answer that," she said. It was the same woman from earlier, whose assertions came by surprise to the gathering of listeners.

"If she loves you, you won't have to ask."

"I agree with you from that standpoint," Shang responded.

He continued to elaborate.

"But I am talking more on the basis of spontaneous head...not head when we about to get it in, but I am talking about head like when we just leaving Walmart, and on the way home while I am driving, I get the urge to want to be pleased at that moment...I mean, if I say '*baby suck my dick*', that's going to come off as degrading or disrespectful to her."

There was a myriad of people trying to restrain, as you could hear broken laughs and suppressed chuckles.

"So how do I ask for head without sounding so degrading?"

A young lady from the audience chimed in... "I understand exactly where you are coming from Shang."

She was one of the spoken word artists on the program.

"My significant other and I have another name for

it. The terminology we use is roses."

Shang had a perplexed look.

"Roses?" He repeated.

"Yea we call it roses....so basically, instead of him saying '*baby can you give me some head or will you suck my dick*', he says, '*baby can I have some* roses'...so when you use that terminology, it is not as degrading or sound as bad. I'm more inclined to do it because it doesn't come off as bad as him saying '*suck my dick*'."

Although she was very candid, the validity of her theory wasn't objected; her point was sensible to the majority, if not all.

"Alright gentlemen, you all heard that right...Just ask for some roses!" Zoella stated jocularly, as she laughed.

"On that note, we are going to take a short break before we finish up the last portion of our discussion."

The show came to a temporary pause, and the DJ immediately sounded the music as everyone enjoyed their cocktails and conversations, ordering appetizers from the light fare menu.

Saturday February 8th 11:56 A.M.

The music was growing louder, as their mincing steps got closer to the threshold of the studio door. They had mixed emotions; feeling giddy and extremely nervous, but yearning to add color to their sexy seductive sides.

Hanging upside down from the vertical pole, she was alerted by the squeaky floors as Hannah and Emma tip toed onto the hardwood pavement.

She took an acrobatic flip off of the pole, landing upright onto her feet.

Saluting them with kindness, "come on in ladies, don't be shy!" her cheerful voice said with a smile. She was graced by their presence.

She took several hurried steps towards the amplifier and turned the knob. The music ceased.

Extending her arm, "hello, I'm Teresa and you are?"

"I'm Hannah," she responded, grasping her hand.

"Oh Hannah! We spoke on yesterday right?"

Showing her megawatt grin, "yes we did!"

"Well I'm glad you decided to come check us out."

"Thank you."

"And who is this?"

"This is my best friend Emma."

Customarily, they greeted each other at the palms.

"Well it's a pleasure to meet you, Miss Emma."

"Likewise!"

Teresa interlocked her hands and assumed an inviting posture.

"Well let me first start off by welcoming the both of you to *KnotEGirl* Dance Studio."

It was a place where women could experience the art of dancing and exercise in a nontraditional, fun exciting way. Teresa, a former stripper that gained notoriety in Las Vegas' most distinguished Strip Clubs, offered flirty fitness classes where girls could learn the basics of pole dancing from simple spins, to choreographing their own strip tease that would leave their significant other lusting for more.

"Secondly, Hannah...Emma. From this day forward, I do not want to see you in my studio again."

Suddenly, they appeared at sea, as they were thrown into a state of disarray by her statement.

She chuckled.

"Meaning, I only prefer to see your alter egos while we are in here. I don't care to see that good girl (air quotes) that momma raised, I want to see that freak that momma never imagined you would become," she said with a wrinkled forehead and raised eyebrows, confirming the accuracy of her explanation.

"So...for now on, in this studio, my name is *not* Teresa. My name is Bambi...okay?"

"Oooo-Kay!" Emma replied with a smile. Hannah

expressed similar affection.

"Okay cool. Now we got that out of the way, just as my name is *not* Teresa at no time in this facility, you are no longer Hannah and Emma. I will not refer to you by your government names ever. So that being said, for the next several moments, as I continue talking to you two about our program, I need you to think of a sexy distinction for me to reference you by…any non-typical name…rather it may be *Pretty Kitty* or *Big Booty Judy*, or whatever. I really don't care. Whatever fits your bad girl persona."

They applauded deep chest laughs and eventually broke loose from all their anxieties as they presumed it would be a fun and friendly session.

"Okay, now another thing I want to go over with you all is our dress code; which there really is no dress code. As long as you have on clothes and are comfortable, then you are okay. The main thing is that I want you to be comfortable and relaxed. And what you ladies have on right now is perfectly fine."

Hannah was wearing black yoga pants, with a Victoria's Secret burnt-orange sleeveless crop top, revealing her sexy tight abs and belly button ring.

Embracing the colors of her Kappa Kappa Gamma Greek organization, Emma had on dark-blue stretch biker shorts and a light blue short sleeved spandex V-neck T-Shirt.

26 minutes later…

It was a dim lit room. They had just finished doing

light cardio and abdominal exercises. The only illumination inside the studio came from colored accent lights. Strangely, they moved in harmony with the melodic tones of Ginuwine's classic R&B slow jam *IN THOSE JEANS* that was blaring in their ears. Devoid of their mates in private, the intimate public environment was bizarre for Hannah and Emma, but they appreciated the ambiance Bambi recreated amidst the setting.

Her eyes examined Hannah. She was impressed.

"That's it *Deep Throat*. Keep doing what you doing!" Bambi blurted, encouraging her efforts and movements.

Blushing and jovial, Hannah exhaled a light giggle, all the while remained tapped into her sensual side.

Unsurprisingly, given the oral treatments she gladly bestowed to her lovers, Deep Throat was the peculiar name Hannah preferred to be called.

Emma was serious; not as playful as Hannah. She was staring at her bodily motions in one of the many wall covered mirrors, concentrating on duplicating Bambi's routine and improving her moves, and hell-bent on conquering the booty shaking game.

"I see you *Wet-Wet*! You're almost there! Just remember to rotate your pelvis!" Bambi shouted as Emma gyrated her hips with both hands on the pole. She was somewhat insecure about her rhythm and stage presence, and felt un-sexy. She never believed she looked seductive while doing it. She was a Caucasian inspired into a realm of twerking by Miley Cyrus, but understood that that domain was widely conventional and more natural for black women.

Exiting the building, Hannah and Emma, side by side, leisurely walked through the parking lot of gravel and rocks. Nashville forecasters correctly predicted the pleasant weather, as the temperature was in the low 60s, with partly sunny skies, and a light breeze of wind at only five miles per hour.

"That was actually a better experience than I thought" Emma mentioned.

After seizing a portion of the protein bar with her teeth, "I know! I really liked it," Hannah's obscured voice muttered, with a mouth full of gristly crumbs. She was on a strict diet, trying to attain a desired size for her upcoming wedding.

Day one was similar to ordinances in traditional school; It was Hannah and Emma's initial occurrence of *KnotEgirl*, where they became acquainted with their instructor and acquired information on what they will gain from the program in its entirety. They mentally digested a small sample, as Bambi catered to them, giving special attention and the right amount of adjustments. After learning three simple pole regimens, Hannah and Emma went from being intimidated by the pole, to pole addicts. They were now antsy to proceed in the nine-session course, all the while repairing their self-image.

"So what do you have planned for the rest of the day?" Hannah asked, as they stood idle between their parked cars.

"Girl nothing really. Probably looking over some of my client's cases."

No longer a real estate paralegal for Jacobs and Collins, she is now a sex crime attorney and just started her own practice in Tennessee and Georgia after graduating from Vanderbilt School of Law and passing the multi-state bar exam. Both Tennessee and Georgia have a reciprocity rule which affords her flexibility to practice law in multiple states.

"Okay cool. Are you all packed and ready to fly out tomorrow?... cause I talked to Sidney last night and she is looking forward to us coming."

Sidney was their other close friend, who is currently in Houston to support her little brother Shawn who will be playing in the *Rising Stars* game later in the night.

"Shoot yea, I been had my clothes ready, what about you?"

"No not yet. But it's only going to take a hot second to find just one outfit. Heck we only staying for a day," she said, shrugging her shoulders.

As usual, through her connections with many pro athletes, Sidney got them tickets to Sundays All Star Game in Houston, Texas.

"Well if you get some downtime and want to get out, just call me okay. Alex is going out with his friends tonight to the Sports Cafe to watch All Star festivities."

"Okay honey I will."

Hannah opened her car door and looked back over her shoulder at Emma.

"Be careful Wet-Wet!" she said, turning the corners of her mouth.

Indulging in laughter, "Whatever! *Deeeeep! Throoooaat!* You got your nerves."

Hannah, punctuating the humor, slowly and artfully inserted the remainder of the protein bar into her mouth, insinuating the depths of her blow jobs.

Emma, couldn't help but to nod her head shamefully before driving away in her sporty candy-red Audi.

Chapter THREE

"Jellybean! I'm ready!"

"Okay Boobie, here I come," Cole responded, lounging against the headboard of his king size bed with his arms crossed. His eyes were channeled on the wall mounted flat screen, relishing re-runs of his favorite sitcom *Seinfeld.*

Slowly, he maneuvered away from the mattress, sliding his feet into his sheepskin house slippers, and advanced towards the restroom. As soon as he stepped onto the Carrara White marble floor tile, he saw his wife, waiting patiently, naked in the tub. He hadn't seen her unclothed in over a month. Ordinarily, their in-house-nurse would assist his wife, but he gave her the day off to attend her son's hockey tournament, as well as next Friday and Saturday for Valentine's Day.

He grabbed the diamond sculpted bath towel from the three-tier rack, and placed it across her back. Rubbing in a circular motion, he absorbed as much water as he could.

"Let me know when you are ready" he said, after

drying her off and placing the towel back on the rack.

"Okay I'm ready," she responded.

He opened the swing door of the walk-in tub and tightly grasped her left wrist. With her right hand, she took a firm grip around the chrome support rail. She was a paraplegic, learning to cope with the everyday struggles of normal activities.

"I'm going to pull you up on the count of three."

"Okay."

"Ready...One...Two...Threeeee," he said, as he forcibly drew her away from the tub seat.

How swiftly the turns of luck can change, it was only three months after their engagement before Jenna, his fiancé, was rear ended last summer on the night of July 4th by a drunk driver. She was severely injured, as her spinal cord was ruptured, causing her to lose sensory and motory functions from the waist down. Nevertheless, due to her physical condition demoralizing her mentally, the joys of planning a large beautiful spring wedding the following year no longer existed. They settled for an intimate October ceremony in his office at the church.

Gradually, he aided her comfortably into her wheelchair.

Holding back his tears, "*Lord, please heal Jenna. Revive the activity of her limbs dear God,*" his grieving voice mumbled under his breath, while pushing her towards the bedroom. Seeing his wife in that condition was mentally and emotionally distressing for Cole and he learned to conceal the depths of his despair while in her presence. He didn't want to deprive her of courage and hope.

He positioned her chair next to the bed where her clothes were and lifted her onto the mattress.

“That's okay jellybean I got it from here,” she said, refusing to accept his assistance with putting her pants on.

She was always an independent woman, and rarely depended on others. And although it wasn't consistent with reality, subconsciously she believed she was more of a burden for Cole rather than his helpmate.

“Boobie, I don't mind. That's what I am here for” he emphasized. Their marriage was loving and solid, but lacked intimacy.

“I know honey I got it. I surely appreciate you” she responded. She wanted to master dressing her lower extremities without a second hand.

“Well let me know if you need anything. I'm about to go downstairs to the study.”

“Okay jellybean.” she said, just as he left the room.

Before attempting to put on her pants, Jenna grabbed the remote and searched her saved DVR listings.

“Yea I’m going to go ahead and watch this right now,” she said aloud to herself, as she clicked on *THE REAL,* a syndicated daytime series themed '*YOU THINK IT WE SAY IT'.* It was her most favorite show that she habitually watched during the day, but she was unable to catch last Thursday afternoon's broadcast. Co-Hosted by *Tamera Mowry-Housley*, *Loni Love*, *Adrienne Bailon*, and *Jeanie Mai*, *THE REAL* brought a distinctive young cultural flavor to their audience.

The best early morning meal in Houston, Texas is at Midtown's *Breakfast Klub* and it was evident as an extended length of people were waiting around the corner on Alabama street. Recognized as one of the better breakfast restaurants in the nation by *Good Morning America*, *USA Today*, and *Esquire*, customary on Sundays, lines at the *Breakfast Klub* were already long with the locals, but considering the All-Star weekend, an abundance of out-of-town guests flooded the building.

Only seconds after blessing their food, "so Deep Throat how was it yesterday at the pole dancing class?" Monica asked nonchalantly, as she raised the fork to her mouth, chowing down on their southern traditional meal *Katfish and Grits.*

Her demeanor was as if the question was conventional.

Mildly shocked, Hannah glanced at Emma before they both erupted in laughter.

Earlier while standing in line, Emma briefly whispered to Monica about their experience at *KnotEGirl*, and graciously shared to her Hannah's alter ego name. From that point, Monica was dying to bring it to Hannah's attention.

"What did you just call her?" Sidney voiced to Monica in a confused tone. She was evidently oblivious, and felt withdrawn from the humor.

"Girl yesterday Hannah and Emma signed up for a pole dancing class and whenever you go to one of them kind of classes..."

"Ahhh, okay-okay! I get it" Sidney responded,

cutting her off. Sidney is very much in the loop with those customs.

After recuperating from laughter.

"*Wet-Wet*! ... and I had a pretty good time yesterday. Thank you very much."

"Alright there now Wet-Wet" Sidney expressed, nudging on Emma's shoulder.

Hilarity lingered amongst the gleeful ladies even as they engaged in artificial fun making of one another. They were all good natured and shared a hearty sisterhood laced with spontaneous amusement.

"Since we talking about names, have you and Terrance figured out what y'all are going to name your baby?" Hannah asked Monica, after taking a bite of her chicken wing.

One of Breakfast Klub's signature dishes, Hannah ordered *Wings and Waffles*, a strawberry topped golden Belgian waffle sprinkled with powdered sugar, it was enclosed by six savory wing pieces.

"Well if it's a boy, we already know we will name him Terrance Anthony Ingram Junior and call him TJ. But if it's a girl we are still pondering over it."

"Do yall at least have somewhat of an idea of what you will name it if it's a girl?" Emma stated.

They are having a surprise gender baby birth and don't want to know until it is born.

"Well he likes the name Terricka, of course because it sort of resembles his name, but I'm not going to say I don't like it, but I am iffy about it...but the name I am leaning towards is Taylor Jade and with that name we can still call her TJ."

"Yea I like that! ...it flows well," Hannah responded.

"Yea me too," said Emma."

"What about you Sidney, what do you think?" Monica asked.

"Yea it's cool. I like that name but I can't help but to think of my client when I hear that name."

"You have a client with that name?"

"Yep."

"So what does she do?"

"She dances" Sidney answered.

"Oh okay that's cool" Monica stated.

"So how long she been dancing for the Pacers?" asked Monica.

Pacemates are dancers for the Indiana Pacers basketball team, and Sidney styles hair for many of them.

Slightly pulling back her lips "she doesn't dance for the Pacers, she dances at the Mirage in Nashville."

Briefly, Monica was calm, quiet, and restrained; momentarily deprived of her conscious.

"At the Mirage!" Monica questioned.

"Yea at the Mirage."

"Uhhh...bitch that ain't dancing that's stripping and hoeing."

The ladies burst a series of chuckles.

With her nose in the air, "Well you can call it what you want to call it; I'm going to be a proud stripping hoe for my husband pretty soon," a dignified Hannah enunciated, embracing her bubbly personality.

"Hey more power to you. At least you know what you are...which is a circumstantial hoe...any who, speaking of pregnancy, what is yall take on Beyonce revealing she's pregnant with twins?"

The girly girls resumed their first meal of the day with laughs, smiles, and the latest celebrity gossip including the tensions and trauma around Amber Heard's & Johnny Depp's divorce and the Oscars blunder, where the wrong name was announced at the show.

Chapter FOUR

Ceremoniously all over the country, Valentine's Day is that time of the year intertwining couples are addressed with the pressures and expectations of the holiday's traditions. Many men express their unsaid feelings of love through a myriad of gifts, chocolates, and eye catching roses while others are nervously rehearsing their proposal speeches so they can deliver those lovely words of '*will you marry me*' precisely from their lips. Women, practically not controlled by tangible obligations, are just simply sporting their stylish evening dresses while hoping their significant other is emotionally and intuitively tuned in throughout the day.

"Give it up for *Tresjee Powers* and *Rudy Francisco*!" said Eddie B, the host comedian out of Houston, Texas.

"Woo-Hoo!" an unspecified person loudly interjected.

Some were brought to their feet, while others remained seated, but there was a widespread full of unrestrained enthusiasm striking their palms together in response to the duets praiseworthy poem.

"Alright, alright. Is everybody enjoying the show so far?" Eddie B asked, surveying the affluent as the atmosphere was now free from noise and agitation.

They expressed their approval.

It was an elegant affair as an array of artists contributed to the venue at RedCat in midtown Nashville. Hannah, navigating around in what seemed to be her tallest stilettos, was dressed in her gray stretch corduroy leggings and a plum linen top with the top two buttons unfastened, exposing curves of her busty breasts. She was figuratively walking on rose petals all day as she was being overflowed with lavish gifts. Earlier at the crack of dawn, her senses were pleasantly disturbed by the sweet aroma permeating throughout the bedroom, waking her from her suspended consciousness. But it wasn't the rectangular bottle of Chanel 5 fragrance she noticed on the side table abutting the bed, rather the strong unique smell of scattered trifoliate jasmine flower leaves surrounding the perfume glass that actually alerted her. Nevertheless, her heart was mostly gladdened by the bouquet of peach roses Alex left waiting on the master bathroom his-and-her sink; each rose wrapped with a $100 bill.

Featured Comedian Gary Owen livened the mood as he executed hilarious routines about Kordell Stewart sending a video of his ass to another man, LeBron James' hairline, and Donald Trump begging people to perform at his inauguration.

"I see all the panty-less ladies in here looking all good and sexy...your man den bought you roses, purses, jewelry, clothes, and brought you here for this show...he den spent his whole paycheck to put a smile on y'all faces."

A swarm of females couldn't resist from drawing back their red colored lips, bracing their selves for a raw, uncensored joke.

"And at the end of the night, after spending hundreds and hundreds of dollars, all he get in return...is some cootie-cat...yea I said it...cootie-cat."

A loud burst of laughs and a series of chuckles followed.

"Fellas, y'all den got creative and spent all this money to get the same exact pussy tonight, that she gave you last night for free."

He continued into another amusing story...

"A retired gentlemen went into the social security office to apply for social security benefits...After waiting in line for hours, they finally called his number to the counter...So when he got to the counter, the clerk asked him for his driver's license to verify his age...he searched in his pockets and realized he had left his wallet at home...So he told the lady he was sorry but he seemed to have left his wallet at home...She then became empathetic because she knew he had waited in line all day and didn't want him to go all the way home and come back to wait again...So the woman said to him 'just unbutton your shirt'...the gentleman opened his shirt, revealing all his curly gray chest hairs...then the woman says 'that silver hair on your chest is proof enough for me'...and she went ahead and processed his application...So when he got home, the man excitedly told his wife about his quirky experience at the social security office...she said 'you should have dropped your pants, you might have qualified for disability too.'"

Throughout the evening, Hannah and Alex watched a breed of rising stars and familiar faces as they devoured cocktails and Italian pastas while laughing the night away.

Meanwhile...

8:01 P.M.

This evening of love was unusual for the newlyweds. Instead of dining at a five-star restaurant and eating overpriced salads, Cole prepared utensil free dinner of caviar, oysters, shrimp, and meatballs with an excess of savory sauces along with a tray of carved fruits. All the while, Jenna was privileged to an hour-long aroma therapy massage in the sun-room, her favorite area of the house. Attempting to keep her spirits lifted, he gave all the solace he could muster to the woman he loved more than life itself; a Givenchy bag and membership for three to an exclusive resort in Montego Bay Jamaica wasn't therapeutic enough. Her depressive illness was hindering her from fully enjoying once-pleasurable activities, including sex. It's been very difficult for her to coexist with her physical condition. Recently diagnosed with psychotic depression, she's never been able to quite regain her emotional balance. And the evolution of their relationship became more and more challenging.

"I don't know what tomorrow will bring. But what I do know is who will bring tomorrow. All I can tell her is that hope is always available through you dear God. Speak through me as I comfort Jenna and encourage her. And make

my words true and valid heavenly father. Be there for my wife exactly where it hurts. Mentally, physically and emotionally. Just be right there God. Heal her from the inside. And if it's in your will, heal her on the outside as well."

"In Jesus name, Amen." he said, concluding his heartfelt prayer just before going into their master bedroom where Jenna was already sleeping. Although the night was mildly romantic, it was totally absent of passion. It's been a long time since he has reveled in the pleasures of sex.

*****

11:56 P.M.

In the candle lit bedroom, the husband and wife-to-be snuggled half naked under the satin sheets, fondling each other's erogenous areas. With their legs tangled up like soft pretzels, they engaged in kinky conversations, voicing their innermost thoughts and feelings in between steamy kisses.

"Damn baby," Alex uttered affectionately after a sizzling kiss. He was pleasantly traumatized.

"Whaaaat?" Hannah asked rhetorically, gazing intensely into his sex craved pupils. By the tone of his voice and his blood-filled crotch against her inner thigh, '*damn baby*' was understood.

"Baby I want to make love to you so bad," he whimpered.

Incredibly horny herself, "I know you do baby and

I want to feel you inside of me. But we only have a few more months until my body is all yours" Hannah empathized, nurturing on his throbbing disc.

Just several weeks ago on New Year's Eve, she made a promise to God that she would abstain from sex until marriage.

Alex exhaled a breath of frustration and rolled over on top of her, diligently gazing down at her unblemished face.

"Well just let me put the head in," he pleaded in such a juvenile pitch, hoping she was intentionally naive.

Her face lit up as the corners of her mouth upturned.

"No Alex...you know good and well that won't happen."

Unable to hold back a smile, "Yes it will," he reiterated unconvincingly.

"Boy whatever."

Absorbed in thought, a sudden idea came to mind. She had a sweet alternative.

"Lay on your back," she commanded in a seductive tone.

He obliged, relinquishing her autonomy.

Hannah straddled across his shins, facing his direction. After slowly removing his Calvin Klein boxer briefs, her fingers crossed over his pubic hairs onto his stiffening erection.

She seized it like a microphone and eye fucked it; a quickie; attentive to the thick vein that bisected his two-toned disc; mostly tan, but closer to pink towards the head.

Ironically, even though she made a promise to God at the beginning of the New Year to abstain from sex until her upcoming wedding, she never assured to him that she wouldn't indulge in oral favors.

Alex slowly drooped his eyelids and settled into the moment, as if he was on his deathbed, anticipating intense pleasure.

She spat on his engorged disc; gave him a very brief hand job; pre-suck procedures.

Again, she spat but more substantially; frothy secretions of spittle bugs scattered over his saliva polished disc.

Wrapping her full delicate lips around the uppermost portion of his manhood, her erotic tongue skillfully maneuvered over his crown.

"Uhn" he acutely groaned, cringing his face. His back arched as she orally massaged him.

She took him in deeper; not far from the shaft and paused. Mentally reciting

One Mississippi, Two Mississippi, Three Mississippi, Four Mississippi, Five Mississippi, Six Mississi...

She gags, ejecting him, saliva dripping down her chin. Exhaling a deep breath, Hannah re-shoved his hardness into her warm mouth; her feverish tongue striking against his disc like sparring motions of a boxer. A blood sport, this was a cum sport. And Hannah, was a knockout artist with the sole intention of putting him to sleep, literally.

Relentlessly she sucked. His moans united with occasional *aahs*, as his body surrendered to the tortuous rhythm of her tongue.

Their eyes met. He was in a state of complete bliss; the imagery of her staring at him seductively while performing fellatio only magnified the feeling.

Hannah took him in even deeper and lingered.

"Ewww Shiiit."

One Mississippi, Two Mississippi, Three Mississippi, Four Mississippi, Five Mississippi, Six Mississippi, Seven Mississippi.

Alex began to grunt and breathe unevenly; constrictions in his chest. Like a respiratory disorder.

Eight Mississippi, Nine Mississippi, Ten Mississippi.

"Aaaahh!" he moaned. He was semi-conscious; scowling; beast-like face.

Eleven Mississippi, Twelve Mississippi, Thirteen Mississippi, Fourteen Mississippi.

He released a series of growing moans as warm heat began surging throughout his body.

Fifteen Mississippi, Sixteen Mississippi, Seve....

"Ahhhh!" He exploded. He was quivering but Hannah didn't pull away. She savored the taste of his sweet nectar.

Hannah discharged his crotch; slouch-jaw; mouth open, in a naughty way; his fantasy slut. White secretions smothered her wagging tongue.

He jerked on his erection; rapid strokes; her pretty face neighboring. She longed for facials.

"Ahhh...Ahhhh!" followed another eruption of creamy fluids onto her cum-filled forehead.

His erection was now feeble and his body was frail; depleted of energy. For the remainder of the night, Alex and Hannah cuddled closely in the bed like babies in dreamless slumber.

The Last Friday in February...

After a sultry live performance by Wes Morgan, a conservatively dressed Pastor Cole stood behind the podium before a roaring, jubilant overflowing crowd of attendees to welcome all visitors.

With gratitude, he verbally expressed his appreciation to all the standing guests being recognized.

Every Friday in February similar scenes play out at Abundant Life church where a few thousand flock to the religious experience themed FAITH FILLED FRIDAYS. The congregation is graced to hear a nationally known gospel artist minister to them in song, before a preached word on faith by one of the most notable Pastor's in the country.

As they were proceeding to sit down on the purple cushioned pew, he extended his hand.

"Wait, Wait!...remain standing. Don't take your seats just yet," he earnestly stated.

"And to prove to you how highly I value your presence, every single last one of you..."

For a hard second, he refrained from speaking. About three dozen stood, not knowing what to expect.

"Will receive a twenty-five-dollar gas card!"

Their excited voices yelled raucously as they were invigorated by his kindness.

He pulled the rubber banded gas cards from his pocket and divided the stack by three.

"Ok will three ushers please come grab some of these to pass around to our wonderful visitors."

They walked towards the pulpit and retrieved their portion to hand out.

With a self-conscious grin, "Okay Zion. I am feeling kind of generous today for some strange reason," he said.

There was a frenzy of *yays*, hand claps and sparkling smiles as they were fully aware of what was getting ready to take place.

"Not this month. Not last week. Not next week. Not on yesterday. Not on tomorrow...but who in here, has a birthday on this exact day?"

Cole couldn't help to notice the woman in the balcony; she burst from her seat, moving her arms and hands freely back in forth bringing attention to herself.

Pointing up in that direction, "we have a winner right up there in the balcony!"

The congregation turned around and looked up; inquisitive to see who Pastor was speaking about.

"Come on down here birthday lady."

She descended down the stairs, holding onto the handrail. She appeared to be in her late twenties.

"Now I am aware that you are a member here

because your face is very familiar. Matter of fact, you always sit up there in that balcony section...don't you?"

"Yes I do," she said, standing next to the communion table. She was wearing a long trendy denim skirt with red leather stilettos, and her waterfall braids were worthy of notice.

"Yea I know. You make sure you sit far, far, far, away from the altar."

She giggled from nervous-embarrassment.

"But unfortunately, your Pastor has a bad memory. So you all just pray for me," he referenced to the assembly of worshipers.

"So tell me, what is your name young lady?"

"My name is Raven."

"Ok Raven. Now you know we are in church. So are you sure today is your birthday?" he asked half-jokingly.

She revealed a friendly smile that exaggerated the beauty of her face.

"Yes."

"What's today's date?"

"I'm just playing, I'm just playing," he interrupted before she could even respond.

Cole had a humorous side to his character that his members warmly embraced.

"No but in all seriousness. How old are you today Raven?"

"I'm forty-one."

Widening his eyes, "forty-one!"

She nodded her head yes.

He was astonished, and so was the congregation taken by surprise as well.

"Well thank God for preserving you because you surely don't look a day over twenty-five...You really don't...not at all."

"Well thank you!"

"Now this is the first and probably the last time I will ever see you this close to the altar, that being said, happy birthday to you Raven. And I wish you many more."

He gave her a crisp $100 bill.

"Thank you," she said with a huge smile as they hugged one another.

She headed back to her seat.

"Alright, alright...we got time for one more."

In deep thought, he had pensive look, with one hand in his pocket and the other holding the microphone; biting his lower lip. It was one of his behavioral habits.

"Okay. Here it is...listen up."

They were eager to hear his proposition.

"Who has...right now in their possession...a paaaaaast due bill...again, a bill that is past due?"

Without the direction of Pastor Cole, the gentleman with neatly ironed khakis began speed walking down the middle aisle.

He reached in his back pocket and handed the folded document to him.

Cole gave him a fraudulent look of shame.

"Jeremy, Jeremy, Jeremy...what do you have here?" he asked, spreading out the paper.

He knew Jeremy very well, as he was a faithful member. A regular bible study participant, he also sung in their 'Psalms of David' choir

"My credit card bill."

After seeing amount due in bold at the bottom right hand corner of the page, he couldn't hold his peace.

"My goodness, what have you bought!" he asked, closely scrutinizing the itemized fee.

The people of faith laughed aloud; Jeremy put a fist over his mouth to keep control of his giggles.

"So you bought an American Airlines flight ticket for $384...What did you do that for?" he asked in a sportive tone.

"Pastor I went home for the holidays in December," he said, with a limp wrist, and the other hand on his hip. He was far from masculine.

Continuing with his interrogation, "Why didn't you pay the bill?"

"Because I am a full-time student and I am not working," he obnoxiously responded. He was a senior at David Lipscomb University, majoring in Social Work.

For a hard second, Pastor Cole gave him a deviltry glare.

"I'm going to pay this bill in the morning."

"Thank youuuuu!" Jeremy said, with a self-satisfied grin. But it was unwelcoming.

"No don't thank me...you just don't get on any more planes...now go back to your seat," he ordered, putting an end to their freewheel conversation.

Proceeding in the worship service, Pastor Cole introduced the speaker of the hour, Dr. Stacy Spencer, the Pastor of New Directions church in Memphis, Tennessee. One of the most prominent preachers in the country, he delivered a tedious sermon from the topic Marvelous Faith. Giving a critical analysis on the story of the centurion man in Luke, the spiritual body voiced their *Amens* and *Hallelujahs* as they were greatly influenced by his proclamation of the word.

Two light taps sounded from his fiberglass door as it was already opened for access. The worship experience concluded and everyone was out of the building except for Naomi and Gary the grounds keeper, who was tidying the sanctuary and ensuring all doors of the building were locked.

Naomi took an initiative step into his office carrying a red shopping bag.

With a cheerful smile, “Well look who's here! ... I never thought you were coming back,” Cole said, casually leaning back in his leather chair with his arms crossed.

“Cole don't even start. I wasn't even gone that long.”

She placed the bag on top of his unkempt desk and sat down in the chair directly across from him.

“So what did you do when you went home?”

“I didn't do much...nothing special. Just visited friends and family and went to daddy's grave site and went over to the church.”

> Their home church was in Atlanta, where Cole formerly served as the Youth and Young Adults Pastor. Naomi was responsible for the Praise & Dance ministry.

“Oh how was it?”

“It was awesome. The guest speaker was Marcus Cosby; he is a biblical mastermind.”

“Oh I don't doubt that one bit. He is a hell of a preacher.”

“And oh yeah, before I forget, sister Madeline was adamant to me about letting you know she is thankful for the card and encouraging letter you sent to Stevie."

She was a long-time member of their home church, whose son was in prison for armed robbery.

"Oh okay cool. Yea I was wondering if he ever received the letter I sent."

Diverting his attention, "So what are you carrying around in this bag here?" he asked, giving it notice.

"Oh it's for you and Jenna."

"Really...awwwwwwwe...I take back everything I said about you over the past few days" he said as he grabbed the corded bag handles.

"Boy whatever."

Reaching his hand into the opening, he pulled out a book.

"That's for Jenna. I remember you told me she enjoys reading."

"Oh, enjoy is an understatement. Reading is who my wife is...Jenna is a page mistress" he mentioned as he skimmed over the synopsis on the back. It was titled RED QUEEN, by Victoria Aveyard.

He placed the book down on his desk and stuck his hand back inside the noisy crinkly bag.

He retrieved a box that was covered in sheet wrap and began to unravel it.

"Ahh Naomi bless your heart! This is what's up right here!" he said with gratitude.

It was a facial grooming kit; bottles of lotions and oils. *SoloNoir* brand, which offered cutting edge skin care coupled with organic ingredients to achieve skin perfection.

"Well I truly thank you and appreciate you. You surely didn't have to do it."

"You welcome. I figured I would be nice and look out for you."

"Well yea, you did look out for me. But I'm not sure if this gift is an indirect way of you telling me I'm unattractive or have bad facial skin or what" he said in a facetious manner.

"O-M-G- Cole, that is not what I was thinking, my goodness."

"Oh okay I was just checking now...people usually aren't nice to me and when they are I get extremely nervous."

Naomi dropped her head shamefully nodding with a lingering smile.

"But on a serious note, I really do appreciate you, not just for this gift but also for all the hard work you do in general for the church. I'm very conscious of it. Trust me it doesn't go unnoticed."

"Why thank you" she responded. It was a prized compliment from her perspective.

He rose from his seat and walked around to the front of his desk, widely opening his arms.

She stood up and embraced him in return. They were snugly, like reacquainting school friends, leaving no space between each other.

"Everything is secure," Gary said as he abruptly strolled into his office; he blanked-faced them.

Taken unaware by his sudden presence, Naomi's eyebrows raised and her lips stretched horizontally. Her back was facing towards his direction.

"Ok well it's time to roll." Cole responded, as they loosened from each other. Although their hug was pure and innocent, anxiety flowed like a muddy river through their bellies.

He grabbed his keys and belongings off of the desk before closing the office door behind him. They paced through the sanctuary towards the main entry, engaging in idle talk. After pressing the buttons on the keypad to set the alarm, they exited the double glass door and went their respective ways.

10:52 P.M.

"Boobie I'm home!" he said aloud, entering through the garage door of his gorgeous 6,000 square foot estate. The structure and enormity of this living space was perfect for their likeness, as Cole and Jenna intended to raise a family with many children when they first built it.

"Hey jellybean" she said, when he appeared in her presence. She was relaxing at the corner end of the brown suede sectional, with her legs stretched out, watching television.

He leaned over and kissed her affectionately on the lips.

"So what have you been doing today?" he asked.

"Oh nothing. I been in the house all day. Talking on the phone and on the computer browsing venues at the resort in Jamaica for us to do."

Putting to use the Valentines gift he bought her, Jenna was enthusiastic about having her best friend Chelsea, and her sister Peggy accompany her on the trip.

"Okay Cool. Did you all figure out when you're going?"

"Yea probably in April, when Peggy's kids go on

spring break. She is planning to have them stay with momma that week."

Peggy is her sister back home in Indianapolis, Indiana.

"Well let me know as soon as possible so I can make plans to drop you off at the airport or anything like that. The spring revival is coming up."

"Okay I will. But you probably will not have to take me. They are actually coming here and we all are just going to leave together and ride in Peggy's car to the airport."

"Okay cool. Whatever works for you."

As the night advanced, Cole and Jenna were curled up on the sofa comfortably, watching TV and engaging in carefree chatter. But with every passing minute, there was a decrease in Jenna's bodily movement and responsiveness.

Her eyes eventually shut and she lost consciousness.

Realizing she was sleep, Cole lifted her from the couch and carried her to the bedroom.

He laid her onto the tempurpedic mattress, partially awakening her.

She pulled the covers over her.

"I'm going to go get your chair and put it next to the bed okay."

"Okay baby. Can you turn on the TV for me?"

He pressed the power button on the remote control before stepping out into the main area. There was something about the artificial light and low noise level Jenna believed was essential for her to gain adequate rest.

Cole returned to the room with her wheelchair, placing it next to the side of the bed where she was laying.

"Goodnight," he said, colliding his lips against her forehead before exiting the room.

An hour or so had elapsed. While watching Criminal Minds, he began to battle the emotion of love for his wife, with his desire for sex; an amenity that didn't seem to fit into their life considering her condition. Although he was anointed and preached the way of holiness in the pulpit, he found himself frequenting a secular luxury, living in the flesh of his porn addiction, engaging in virtual sexapades.

He logged onto the desktop computer in the home office. In the web browser, he typed *cherokeesfetishes.com* where a bevy of playmates awaited him on that site, but Cherokee D'ass was preferred above all others.

"I love the things you do with your tongue," his voice trembled, after she skillfully tied the cherry stem into a knot with her tongue.

They routinely began their conversation with

sweet nothings and not-so-dirty phrases.

Her eyes burning into his lust clouded blue eyes, “I'm sure you do daddy,” she responded.

“Now touch yourself and let me watch.”

He fondled his hardening sex muscle, through his cotton pajama pants; Alexander Olch brand. He was shirtless; bareback. Physique like Mark Wahlberg.

“Do you like it when I touch myself here?” she asked, staring into his desirous eyes.

He nodded his head yes.

“Yea I know you like this juicy pussy. That's why you keep coming back for more, ain't that right daddy?”

“No doubt. You know I can’t resist.”

Their correspondence over the web grew provocatively, and the explicit images she displayed to him were a source of stimulation.

“Baby, you have to follow all my rules tonight okay?”

“Okay. You call the shots.”

There was a brief moment of silence, as they stared at each other; their minds drifting through sexual perversions.

Her tongue coasted her crimson red lips.

“Pull out that big dick and stroke it...like you would if you were fucking me in my ass.”

Removing his pants, he began masturbating to the visual aid and his overactive imagination, anxious for his pending orgasm.

“And you dare not cum until I tell you to.”

Living vicariously through Cherokee fantasies was beginning to escalate from an occasional vice to a full blown addiction, and the holy spirit that dwelled inside alerted him of his guilty pleasures. And even though he felt devilish and wicked, he knew that his sexual appetite left unsatisfied could potentially turn vengeful. Subconsciously, Cole absolved himself for this particular unjust behavior because it was his personal defense mechanism against adultery.

Chapter FIVE

The Following Tuesday Afternoon.

Walking up to the attendant behind the glass window, "Yes, I would like one for Get Out at 2:05 please."

She swiped his card and handed him a printed ticket.

"Thank you sir, enjoy your show," said the attendant.

Cole proceeded into the theatre solo. Even though he had an extremely busy social calendar, he always made sure to include me-time into his schedule. For him, accompanying himself enabled him to tune into his emotions and personal interests which was vital for him maintaining a fulfilling life.

Aside from popcorn, a large coke, green apple flavored sour straws and all the sugar intake, it was two hours well spent. The film was phenomenal and never felt dull or lifeless. It brazenly displayed to the audience oversimplified perceptions, racism, interracial dating stereotypes, unspoken dialogue amongst blacks, with a sufficient amount of humor and suspense laced in the storyline. In the grand scope, it portrayed stellar performances of fascinating characters. Although it was a tad bit flawed in its larger portrait, for better or worse, it possessed all the hallmarks of a trophy winner.

"Hey Pastor!" someone yelled, just as he began walking on the parking lot pavement. It was a familiar voice.

He glanced over his left shoulder and turned around.

"Oh hey there Gabby how are you doing?"

"I'm good!" she responded, wearing a broad smile.

"Hey buddy you doing okay?" he asked, initiating their fist bump greeting. It was her 13-year-old son.

"Yeah."

Gabby gave him a stern look, "boy you know how to speak better than that."

"Yes sir," he responded a second time.

"Gabby if you don't leave him alone. He's okay."

"Pastor I just like for my child to be respectful that's all."

Coming to the boy's defense, "he's not being disrespectful! Good Lord O Mighty."

"Besides, I don't like to be called Sir. It makes me feel old."

She blank-faced him.

"By the way, I don't want to hold you up, but I just wanted to tell you that your message on healing this past Sunday was right on time and well received because mommy is now cancer free!"

"Well praise God! I take delight in the news!" an enthusiastic Cole expressed aloud.

"Thank you! Momma told me she watched you online and she could just feel the Holy Spirit moving on her while lying in the bed."

"Well that is wonderful. Tell your mother I am happy for her and now that she is healed, she needs to get back in that kitchen and bake me up a pecan pie."

They briefly giggled.

Patting him on the back, "so thank you for all your prayers and for coming up to the hospital to check on her. We really appreciate you!"

"Awww don't thank me. Give your praises to God because he deserves all the credit."

"Most Certainly."

"Well let me stop running my mouth so we can get in here and catch this movie," said Gabby.

"Okay Gabby. Will I see you tomorrow at midweek bible study?" he asked in a mocking tone.

Curving the corners of her mouth, "No comment" she said, and walked away.

*****

Seated sluggishly, Cole delayed starting the ignition. He was lacking liveliness. Insanely jealous; pondering over his unsatisfied hopes.

"I pray for everyone…constantly…and they get healed. But my own wife can't get an ounce of restoration in her body" he said, shaking his head regrettably.

The past several months had been spiritually draining. It was difficult for him as a shepherd to lead the flock of Abundant Life, considering he was slowly tip toeing through his own valley of death.

He assumed a menacing disposition. A ticking bombshell. Wide eyed, with a sinister glance into the windshield.

Striking the steering wheel, "What the fuck!" he angrily expressed aloud, harboring animosity towards the creator himself. Capricious mood swings were a natural occurrence.

An indefinite number of minutes elapsed as he was slumped down in the seat. Discouraged; struggling to cope with his own grief.

Cole assembled his emotional beads back on their string and drove away, listening to a Christian soundtrack. Within the trenches of a heartache, he finds hope in gospel music. And Cole knew he had no choice but to press on.

Thursday March 20th, 3:56 P.M.

It was late afternoon in the spring. The weather was warmer, golden leaves were being swept across lawns by brisk winds, and plants were beginning to revive. In the same fashion, so was Alex and Hannah, sharing a feeling of growth and renewal as they drove down the main road of the superb Green Hills housing edition, where homes ranged from 400k up to 1 million dollars. Zoned to the best of schools, Shorelake Tahoe was a one of a kind community featuring resort style amenities which included two swimming pools with slides, a splash-pad, tennis courts, a fabulous fitness center, and an elegant banquet hall.

Alex parked his Infiniti Q45 in front of the gorgeous model home.

Side by side, they walked down the stoned pavement that parted the yard of planted flowers, shrubs, and a palm tree.

“Hello Alex and Hannah,” said Bradley, the on-site realtor.

In a jolly tune “hey-hey” she responded.

Although they aren't jumping the broom until later in the fall, opting to buy a home was the next logical step after their engagement. Not to mention, this shared venture into home ownership seemed to strengthen their bond over the past few months.

"Why don't you all come into my office and have a seat."

An experienced realtor, Bradley was tall, pale-skinned and slender; golden hair; in his early to mid-40s.

"Can I get you guys any water?" he asked, as they sat down in the chairs in front of his desk.

"Sure" said Alex.

"Hannah how about you?"

"Yea I will take one as well."

He handed both of them a Nestle bottled water.

"So what did you guys decide?" Bradley inquired.

Even though they came to an agreement to build their first home in this particular neighborhood, they had been indecisive on a floor plan to settle with. There was a surplus they could choose from, and they eventually narrowed it down to three. This appointment was the pre-scheduled day for them to make their final decision on a floor plan and lot location.

"We decided to go with the Capistrano."

The Capistrano floor plan was exactly 5,748 square feet. It had a wide-open family room with soaring ceilings. The large kitchen was graced with hardwood floors along with a breakfast bar. And the downstairs expansive master suite had a sitting area and in the elegant bathroom were marble floors and a Jacuzzi tub. Upstairs were spacious secondary bedrooms, a large game-room, media room and an additional flex space for fun or relaxing.

"Cool...the Capistrano is our second most sought after floorplan behind the Bellaire. But for me personally, it's my favorite," said the realtor.

"Well all I need from you guys now is your escrow deposit to get the building process going and for you to look at this map of our open lots and pick where you want your home to be."

After handing them the neighborhood cadastral map, Hannah began looking over it as Alex was writing out a check for 25k.

"And tell me what your schedules are like for next week, so I can book your spot at the design center."

Alex gave him the check and then glanced over at Hannah. Because he was self-employed, he left it up to Hannah to determine the day.

"Ummmmm...How about next Friday after four-thirty. Is that open?"

"Let me call over there and ask Veronica."

He retrieved the landline phone from his desk and dialed the number.

"I think this is the lot we should go with right here?" said Hannah, pointing it out to Alex on the map.

His eyes followed her index finger.

"Alright that's cool. You know it doesn't make me any difference. If that's where you want to build, then that's where we will be babe."

Reacting favorably, she smiled at him as she rubbed his thigh.

Bradley placed the cordless phone back on the base.

"Okay guys. I got you set up to be at the design center next Friday at Five-Thirty with Veronica."

"Great! That's fine."

Now let's go over your contract and let me explain to you all the specifics.

An hour or so had elapsed. Alex and Hannah left feeling warm and fuzzy, as they knew they were one step closer to entering the realm of home ownership and building their nest.

6:08 P.M.

"May I take your order please?" The young lady asked over the intercom. They were waiting in the drive thru lane at Dairy Queen. Her most preferred above all fast food eateries.

"Baby what you want?"

"Uhhh...Get me a butterfinger blizzard treat."

"Yea let me have a butterfinger blizzard treat." Alex said to the cashier.

"What size do you want that in?"

"Medium." Hannah said.

"Uh...make that a medium please."

"Okay does that complete your order?"

"Yes ma'am."

"Your total will be $4.28. Pull around to the next window."

Buzz Buzz Buzz his phone vibrated just as he released his foot off the brake pedal.

Glancing at the screen, he realized it was his sister and had a sudden slight inkling that something was wrong. It was very rare for her to call him to just engage in idle conversation.

"Hello."

"Hey Alex."

"Hey Abigail what's going on?"

"Did you hear what happened to Austin?"

She had dullness to her voice.

"No what happened?" Alex asked.

Austin is their younger brother who is a high school senior.

"He was arrested earlier today for rape."

In a tone of uncertainty, "Huh? He was arrested for rape?"

"Yea."

"What do you mean he was arrested for rape?"

Alex was mystified.

"I don't know all the details. He was just arrested earlier today down there in Atlanta. I guess he went to some party last night and took part in a gang rape...supposedly the girl was drunk."

"So he's in jail in Atlanta?"

"Yea...and they have it on video. One of the guys at the party was being silly and recorded it. The video went viral and got back to her parents. The girl is fifteen. And they trying to prosecute him on statutory rape...He's facing up to ten years."

Alex had a lump in his throat; he exhaled a frustrating sigh.

"Okay. Alright let me call you back and see what's going on" he said before ending the call.

"Who was that?" a concerned Hannah asked.

"That was my sister. She just told me that Austin got arrested."

Alex rolled down his window and retrieved the ice cream from the cashier.

They pulled off.

"What did he get arrested for?"

"For raping some fifteen-year-old girl in Atlanta.

She said it was like a gang rape."

"Oh no!"

The remainder of the ride home was quiet. Alex could only think about what he could do to help and how he could have prevented it. The news was mentally taxing. He felt partially responsible for his brother's actions.

They arrived at Hannah's place. Alex was still calm. Exhibiting a quiet strength. But he could no longer subdue his emotions. He was rattled to the core.

"Come here baby." Hannah said, as she cradled him in her arms. Alex was sitting on the couch; tears flowing down his cheeks. The internal pain was acute. This was one of the rare times Hannah ever saw Alex cry like this. He was devastated. Shedding tears uncharacteristically. He had a very high pain tolerance. But that was in the game of football and conditioning. He could push through the distresses of a training regimen above any other athlete in the state. Absolutely no one out worked him. But this infliction was indifferent. He never had a family member taken away from him so suddenly. This loss he never imagined enduring.

Friday, 1:48 P.M.

It was almost midafternoon. Jenna had just finished her first meal of the day; a sausage, potato and cheese omelet. She had a lackluster morning, as she stayed up in the bedroom watching the past few episodes of *THE BACHELOR* that she prerecorded. She was out of town in Chicago rehabbing, and during that period of time she wasn't able to tune in.

Let me get in here and book my flight and make preparations for the trip she thought to herself.

In her electric wheelchair, she strolled through the front room and then made her way into the home office. She moved the roller chair away from the desk.

Jenna logged onto the computer and started probing around the web for interesting venues to solicit as well as activities to engage in for their upcoming vacation to the Bahamas. After about a half hour of researching, she bookmarked a food tour, boat tour, Nassau Museum, parasailing, wellness spa and casino.

"That should be good for right now. I will call

Chelsea and Peggy later on to see what else they have in mind to do," Jenna said aloud to herself.

"Let me see what these flights are looking like on cheaptickets.com."

She started typing in the browser; floating on air; intoxicated on her own high spirits.

WWW.CHE

Jenna paused; stopping her fingers from hitting the keys. The web address www.cherokeesfetishes.com popped up just as she manually inputted the letters CHE.

What is Cherokees Fetishes? She thought to herself.

Leaving almost nothing to the viewers' imagination, the homepage of Cherokee was visible on the screen with links *Members Area* and *Live WebCam* displayed. Jenna quickly realized that it was an adult website.

She was extremely suspicious; her thoughts were jumbled. But she knew it wasn't coincidence this web-page came up. It was in the browser history, which is why it automatically appeared after she began to type the first three corresponding letters.

Jenna naturally became uneasy. And to a small degree insecure about her own race as a Caucasian even though she had stunning looks with an alluring smile. She didn't want to accept her intuition. Her inkling was to give Cole the benefit of the doubt. In all the years of knowing him, she was never lead to believe he was fascinated with lurid material; black women. They have always been very open with each other; lack of secrecy if any; willing to share their most private matters. She rationalized him bringing his interests for porn to her attention because in her mind he had no reason to hide it; she always sympathized and tolerated much more than any typical woman. But she also trusted her own judgment and didn't put it past him.

Jenna diverted; concentrated on booking flight tickets; she was in a rare good mood for a change. She's been hauling around a lot of emotional baggage and didn't want to spoil her vibe. She just put it deep in her recollection for right now.

The following Friday Afternoon…March 28th

Thanks to her battery powered partner, Hannah laid in the bed momentarily feeling relieved and reinvigorated. Courtesy of Alex ordering her a personalized 20-ounce coke bottle with her name on it, along with *Dexie-Berries* edible arranged chocolate covered strawberries he sent to her office, her hormones were volatile by the mind-altering gesture, so she rushed home after work to pacify those steamy desires.

Staring into her closet Hannah let out a dramatic sigh, contemplating on what she was going to put on. She was a shopaholic; she could never resist a bargain. At least one-third of her merchandise still had tags on them. And more than half of those were from Dillards and Bloomingdales.

Hannah decided on the less wrinkled shirt and her favorite leggings, sliding on cute flats; It was like the window to her soul. She felt relaxed but hurried, because Alex was on his way to pick her up for their appointment at the design center.

The two-car-garage door lifted; it had a distinct sound. Hannah knew it was Alex, but as usual, she wasn't quite ready.

"Hello." Hannah said, answering her phone.

"I'm outside."

"Okay here I come."

About four, maybe five minutes elapsed. But it felt like twenty minutes for Alex. And only 30 seconds for Hannah. She was applying a touch of makeup.

Her phone chimed. It was Alex's ringtone.

"Hey I'm coming right now," she said just as she answered.

"Damn honey what the fuck are you doing...We need to go." Alex irritably expressed.

Hannah hung up the phone; threw on her dazzling accessories. She stole a glance in the mirror before perfuming herself with the Chanel 5 he bought her for Valentine's Day.

*****

She wasn't fully dressed unless she was wearing a smile; a vigorous Hannah flounced through the garage sporting stylish Bvlgari sunglasses; her hair in a bun.

"Hey" she said after pulling shut the passenger door of his Infiniti Q45.

"Hey."

He had an uneven temperament.

Rubbing his groin, "baby what's wrong?" she asked blithesomely.

"Nothing."

"You sure?"

"You want me to suck your dick?"

She began to grope him.

"You want me to make you a sandwich…talk to me." she said in such a carefree tone.

He gave her an evil eye; counterfeit. Hannah knew she managed to lighten his mood.

Unveiling a cheesy smile, she burst into laughter.

Alex shook his head; never saying a word. He knew in his heart of hearts she would go down on him with gratitude.

"Put your seat belt on with your crazy ass."

He switched the gear from park and sped off.

*****

Leaving out of the design center, it was now dark. The sun had already set. Their appointment lasted much longer than they anticipated. They had to choose from a variety of countertops, cabinets, appliances along with details from mosaic backsplashes, stainless steel sinks and chrome faucets. And even though they were there for an extended time, Alex and Hannah were not quite able to agree or decide on all features for their home. They prearranged another meeting to return in a few weeks to finish what they started.

Alex pulled up in front of the condo and put the car in park.

"Baby we need to talk."

"What's going on?" Hannah anxiously responded.

Alex was mentally uneasy himself, certain that she wouldn't receive his sentiments well.

He exhaled a long deep breath. His palms were sweaty.

"Given that we are building this house, getting married, and making a lot of huge purchases in unison for now on, I think it is best we talk about money strategies and our respective contributions for the household."

For a lot of engaged couples, conversing about money is taboo. They are either hesitant or oblivious to broach the topic of merging finances; a discussion that can make or break their marriage.

"Okay. That's fair."

"So, tell me what's on your mind...what's your thought process?"

Money talks, love listens. Hannah and Alex engaged in healthy, open dialogue about their respective roles and how they would secure their future. They learned that they both actually had similar money methods and viewpoints and when Hannah suggested that she wanted to help control the household finances, Alex agreed without feeling he was being undermined as the man of the house. They were hands on about everything, including their credit scores and debt, and they accepted each other's imperfections. Alex's credit score was at a 790, where Hannah's was a 650. But Alex had a substantial amount of more debt than Hannah, considering he got a loan from the bank to open up his car rental business.

"Fuck you! I'm done talking about this shit!" Hannah screamed. She was enraged with a raw anger. Nothing can kill romance faster than a prenuptial agreement. Their conversation quickly went from pleasant and peaceful to a verbal dispute as Hannah learned that Alex was hesitant to seal their union without it.

She got out of the car and slammed the door; walking through the garage at a furious pace.

Alex wasn't the type of guy to fuss and fight. He never intended to stir up tension even though he was finite on his stance. He was raised to either kill you with kindness or battle with attorneys. He felt that because

Hannah's perception of prenuptial agreements has been perpetuated by the media and headline-generating celebrity divorces, she wasn't willing to accept his position and understand how she could actually benefit from it as well. He argued that it was smart estate planning and many financial and legal experts strongly suggest prenups, and wanted her to not look at it as an unromantic jinx. But Hannah wasn't buying it. She transmitted his perspective as a lack of trust and him pre-planning a divorce.

After assuring Hannah made it in the house, Alex drove away. He was disgruntled, feeling like one of her students. There wasn't a cheat sheet permitted for this test. Even though his full disclosure eventually sparked up a heated verbal dispute, his attitude about it was steadfast. He knew that a prenuptial agreement would prevent headaches brought on by potential heartaches.

Chapter SIX

Saturday, April 5th

After untying the nylon apron from around his neck, he gave Cole the hand mirror.

Scoping the entirety of his head through the oversized mirror behind him, he was satisfied with the arrangement of his hair as he opted for his signature mid-tier fade, tapered at the temples, accentuated with his beard and mustache perfectly trimmed, giving him a balanced and flattering look.

He stood up from the chair feeling refreshed, with a little bit less chestnut blonde hair.

"Keep the change," he said, as he gave the barber a $50 bill.

A detailed wash of his sporty jaguar and a stop at The Gentlemen's Salon was his Saturday domestic routine. It was like a cult institution in the southern capital and different from all other salons. Because it was open 24 hours, it catered to night owls as well as those who worked odd hours and traveled red eye. Clientele typically consisted of truck drivers, club musicians, and exotic dancers.

"Thanks Rev." I appreciate you.

After downing a stiff drink, "Is that the Rev I see over there?" someone shouted from across the shop with a billiards stick in his hand. A section of the establishment was furnished with pool tables and arcade games to entertain customers while waiting.

Cole glanced in that direction. He didn't know his name but he had fair knowledge of him given he was a regular patron.

Cole raised a clenched fist.

"Rev I saw you in Passion City the other day."

Suddenly, it was a laugh-filled environment as they were amused by his statement. Passion City was a popular strip club in Nashville.

Cole depicted a baffled expression.

With a lingering smile, "Naw, naw, not literally, but like on the big screen TV. No lie. I was watching the newscast on channel twelve, eating my chicken wings. Then when the news went off, your service came on."

Cole's sermons broadcasted locally every late Saturday night.

"I started feeling kind of weird for a second. I'm

looking up at the TV and the scripture displayed across the screen, but in the corner of my eye, I see this ass twerking on stage."

His statement provoked raucous laughter amongst the affluent.

A place where unique bonds are birthed, not only will you overhear the buzz of clippers, but you can also receive the latest gossip news and catch collective conversations that cater to masculine tastes in the African American barbershops.

"What was the sermon subject?" Cole asked, questioning the veracity of his account.

"Uh oh," intervened the brother standing against the wall, next to the table of scattered *Essence*, *Jet*, and a *Straight Stuntin* Magazine featuring *Ms. Cat* on the cover. He was shouldering a big black bag, with incense and knock-off colognes he pushed to customers.

Snapping his fingers, "umm...ummm," he uttered while trying to recollect his thoughts.

"It was...it was...Finding God in the Dark."

Cole raised his eyebrows, nodding his head affirmatively.

"Yea, yea, you all thought I was lying why y'all laughing."

"Whatever Omar don't nobody care" Tessa mentioned in a playful tone. She was the only female barber present.

"Besides, what's a married man doing in the strip club anyways?"

"What you think...I was looking at them fat ol asses shake," he said.

An assemblage of customers burst loud sounds and chuckles at the inanity of his words expressed.

"There ain't nothing wrong with me going to a strip club as a married man."

"Whatever Omar you know better than that!"

"No I don't!" he responded.

"Okay, well answer me these questions."

"You consider yourself a Christian right?"

"Most definitely."

"Okay well then, would you do it in front of Jesus?" Tessa asked.

Repeating her question, "Would I do it in front of Jesus."

"Ummmm...I wouldn't fuck my wife in front of Jesus but that don't make it wrong."

Several customers instantly began clutching their stomachs, gulping for air, collapsing into a fit of hysterical laughter.

"Am I right Pastor!" he shouted, staring at Cole. He unveiled a hearty smile.

"I have no comment" Cole responded as he

began to exit towards the door.

Somehow to Cole, his presence seemed to occasionally draw fascinating dialogue between sports, women, religion, race, and sex amongst the brethren. And even though he was reluctant to engage, deep down inside, he always enjoyed the ambiance and camaraderie in this place of business.

Cole received a text message, as he was driving down interstate 65, en route to the church.

[Jenna-9:03 A.M.]~~**We just landed in Jamaica. Just letting you know. I will call you once we get settled into the room.** :-*

[Cole-9:03 A.M.]~~**Okay baby. Yall have fun and be safe. I love you.**

[Jenna-9:04 A.M.]~~**I love you too.**

He scanned his twitter timeline. He tweeted a flyer advertising worship service in the morning as well as a quick live video on Instagram.

Connecting the auxiliary cord with his smart phone, he began to play Jason Crabb's single, 'Midnight Cry'; a former Grammy award winning gospel artist.

Oh yea, let me text Naomi back he thought to

himself. He had a habit of texting and driving.

[Cole 9:07 A.M.]~~**Of course. You know I am not passing up any dishes you cook.**

She asked him if he wanted her to bring him a plate later in the afternoon.

9:48 A.M...

"Man! Those are the bomb!" he said aloud to himself after eating four yeast donuts. He had been to many pastry shops around the country, but by his estimation, Longs Bakery of Indianapolis, Indiana was by far the best. Jenna's sister brought him a box, as he begged her the day before. Prior to getting on the freeway to Nashville, she made a stop in Haughville neighborhood to get him a dozen.

"Okay now I can re-focus."

The Mercy Hospital, The Hospital of Incurables Pastor Cole wrote down on his notepad. He was outlining his sermon for the upcoming Sunday.

He continued in forming words on the paper.

1. The Patients That Are Admitted

A) A Blind Man

B) A Diseased Woman

C) A Demonized Daughter

Although he was exerting himself via his spiritual calling, jotting down comments, flipping through passages in the synoptic gospel, his body was craving for intimacy and his conscious thinking was being shaped by deep imaginations imbedded in his heart.

2. The Available Physician he wrote.

A man normally guided by the counsels and influences of the Holy Spirit, he was distracted by lust.

A) He Will Take Any Patient

Mentally engrossed in fantasy, he proceeded in preparing his message.

A few endless minutes elapsed after he browsed and read over the fifth chapter of Mark.

With an overstimulated brain, he noted...

B) He Will Treat Any Problem

His anxieties were irrational; he was fidgety; experiencing sexual thoughts.

Fortunately, but unfortunately, his optical pleasures were just a few clicks away.

He grabbed his iPhone that was near the edge of his desk and thumb pressed the safari icon, opening up the bookmarked website: *xvideos.com*

After fumbling through his drawer for the remote control, he hit the power button, turning on the wall mounted HDTV straight ahead of him.

Via air drop, Pastor Cole connected the web page, allowing the content to be shown on the flat screen television.

He typed *Layla Monroe* in the search engine.

A multitude of video links flashed on his touchscreen.

Randomly, he selected the third image.

As the music sounded and the footage appeared on the HDTV, he used the remote to turn down the speaker volume low enough for his ears only. But not before putting his bible away in the bottom drawer. Although he was in the church office, oddly, he wasn't fearless enough to watch raunchy smut videos with the sacred book in plain sight.

Dressed in her red body stockings and high heels, a short sequence of images processed before Layla

Monroe threw her luscious lips on his rigid penis. She was an enthusiastic oralist with a gravity defying bubble butt. And Pastor Cole was gazing heavily from his leather chair, living vicariously through the experience. And even though preaching was his first love, over time, porn heightened to a distant second. His addiction became so problematic that he was now violating the sanctity of the church without guilt.

Picking up his phone, Pastor Cole placed his index fingertip on the tiny oval icon and drug it to the right; releasing at 11:36.

He put the phone back on the desk. He was now hands free, pampering his increasing erection through the thin sweat pants he wore; absorbing Layla Monroe's freakish moans and large areolas as she gyrated backwards on her bed mate's cock.

The door swung open, triggering his nervous system.

"Hay-hay," a vibrant Naomi said, bursting into the office.

He was spooked, as if he had seen a ghost.

"I brought you some chicken jambalaya."

"Okay," he said. He was extremely tensed, reaching his jittery hand across the desk to grab the iPhone.

With the phone now in his grasp, the screen displayed > slide to unlock, as Naomi laid the aluminum foil wrapped plate on his desk.

"Now you may have to warm it up in the microhhh..."

Naomi appeared bamboozled, hearing sounds suggestive of sexual activity. She slowly turned around, and her eyes confirmed what she heard.

"What the heck" she uttered, just as Cole was punching in the passcode on his phone.

She revolved her head back towards him; he stopped the video.

Laying his phone back on the desk, a self-conscious Cole lowered his forehead into the palm of his hand.

After what seemed to be an endless moment of silence, he exhaled a deep breath.

With dullness in his voice, "Hey Naomi, shut my office door and have a seat. I need to talk to you for a second."

Although he preferred the anonymity, he had no choice but to be forthcoming after being caught red handed.

She closed the office door and sat back in the chair across from him. She had an uneasy calmness to her.

Like a catholic boy confessing his sins in the presence of a priest, Cole qualmishly articulated to Naomi his trying situation, explaining how it lead to a fascination of watching grunt filled sexual encounters of women leaving slimy messes at the climax of their scenes.

"Well Cole I understand your predicament. I really do. It's no biggie as far as I am concerned. For a man to go as long as you have without sex is a tough stretch."

Trivializing his sacrilegious acts, her response was somewhat unanticipated.

"You disclosing this to me does not change how I view you as a Pastor and most importantly you can guarantee that it's between me and you."

Cole felt relieved by her reassurance of confidentiality which was extremely vital to him. Even though he was outgoing, zealous and loved by the parishioners who sat under his charismatic preaching, what they didn't see beneath his anointed spiritual gift and successful ministry was the hidden depths of his heart.

"Because at the end of the day, you are my longtime friend first and Pastor second. And the same way you have always made yourself accessible to me when I needed to vent and never judged me, I have no problem doing the same for you."

Over the years his friendship was a shelter for her storms of life.

"Well I truly appreciate your compassion and sympathy. I don't take it lightly."

"Oh no problem. You know I got your back Cole."

"Matter of fact, lets hug it out."

Scooting the chair back, she stood up and extended her arms.

"Come give me a hug" Naomi said, revealing her glorious smile. A sweet Georgia peach, she had an infectious personality and her beauty commanded attention.

He strolled around his desk. They inter-meshed with one another; amicably.

"Let me know how that chicken jambalaya taste. I spiced it up for you because I know you like spicy foods" Naomi said, after they disengaged from one another.

"Oh yea no doubt. I already know you did your thang."

Because his wife was on vacation, he gave their in-home-nurse the week off. Often when she doesn't cook, one of the members on staff will prepare him a meal for that day.

"Well I am not going to trouble you any longer. I know you are hungry, so go ahead eat your food. I was just dropping by to bring you your plate. I need to hurry up and go run some errands before this traffic hits."

"Okay Naomi...see you this Sunday" he said, escorting her to the door.

He turned the knob and pulled it open for her.

With a stern gaze, "Hey thanks again for all you do."

By the look on his face, she could sense that he assessed her very highly.

They re-embraced at the threshold of the door. But this hug was meaningful; lacking social graces. With her face buried in his neck, her perfume and generosity sparked an automatic reaction in his briefs that she clearly felt against her body. And even though their relationship was always platonic, Naomi found herself being turned on by the reality of the man who is usually praying for her, seems to be preying on her.

Naomi separated her face from his chest and tilted her head back slightly.

Their eyes met.

She gave him a cautious stare; sharply penetrating his blue eyes.

He drew nearer to her, tentatively. Their lips hesitated to touch. Cole was feeling as if his nerves were like strings being tightly stretched on a violin.

Choosing the lesser of the two evils, he collided his lips with her caramel dimpled cheek. It was a more befitting kiss. Nevertheless, the offerings of carnal temptations amongst them was more than offerings on Easter Sunday. This kiss, for Naomi, was an unforgettable kiss. It was a kiss with potential. A kiss that garnered possibilities. A kiss that threatened to open the floodgates of intense passion.

Coming to their senses, she freed herself. Moved back one step; giving them breathing room. Cole's world became a Seahawks fan. Superbowl 49. Goal line interception. He had a dubious distinction.

"Well...umm," she said. It was a mysteriously strange aura between them. Temporarily insane, Cole began digging in his pockets for a nonexistent item.

"I...think...I'm going to go ahead and go," said Naomi, feeling imprisoned by the moment. She didn't know his state of mind. Neither was he quite sure of hers. All he knew is that he wanted a replay. Not the kind where you relive the previous sequence in slow motion, but the kind when both teams commit a penalty; a replay of downs.

"O...kay...I...ummm...will...see ya...some other time." Cole responded in disbelief.

Naomi gaited down the hallway and out of the building.

Declaring himself guilty, Cole leaned his head against the wall. Eyes shut. Humbly posturing his heart before God.

"Heavenly father I have found the woman I will love and honor for the rest of my life. In sickness and health. Til death do us part. I promise no other will ever distract me again nor have my attention. Lord I need you to forgive what I have just done. I devote myself to you God and love and cherish Jenna as my one and only. I beg you Lord to intercede.

Save what we have built and help me to grow stronger and to continue being the man and husband she so deserves."

He paused; gathering his thoughts.

"Please God. Save our love. And please, please, please, answer my prayer of healing for her. At times, my heart crushes inside my chest seeing her like that. My lungs suffocate with no oxygen. I hurt for her. And I love her and will continue to be faithful and devoted to my wife. I know there is hope for us. And that hope is all because of you. So please God. Just help me. Help us. Heal my Jenna Lord God. I can't live without her. She is the woman for me. She is my forever. Please help me God. I won't give up. My heart is true. My love is real. And I will never give up. This I promise. Amen."

Chapter SEVEN

The following Friday...

"Girl that is crazy that they trying to convict Austin like that!" Sidney stated.

"I hope they just dismiss the case. It ain't that deep. Kids are going to be kids."

Killing two birds with one stone, they were joy riding down i-75 South in route to Atlanta in Sidney's luxurious pearl white, fully equipped Range Rover; thanks to the generosity of her brother Shawn. They had floor level tickets to the Atlanta Hawks vs Memphis Grizzlies game, also courtesy of Shawn, which was their initial purpose for the weekend getaway. But considering that Hannah had yet to say *YES* to the most important dress she would ever wear, her entourage came up with the idea to help her shop around Atlanta for her gown.

"Yea that's what we bargaining for. Hopefully at worse he can get off with a misdemeanor." Emma responded. She was Austin's attorney, Alex younger brother, who was in a battle with the state of Georgia for rape of a minor. Austin is 17 and his accuser is only 15, and according to Georgia law, 16 is the legal age a minor can consent to sex.

"Yea I'll just keep praying for him."

"*YOUUU* going to pray for him?" Hannah asked Sidney, with appalled sarcasm.

She was sitting in the backseat, watching *GabeBabeTV* on her iPhone; a YouTube channel that was her favorite pass time.

Sidney took her eyes off the road and stared at Hannah in the rearview mirror; grinning.

"What's that supposed to mean!"

She was pleasurably-offended.

"Girl I'm starting to think you an Atheist. You haven't been to church in like forever have you."

"Whatever Hannah!" she responded, even though Hannah's remarks resonated with her. Sidney felt blameworthy, as she has prioritized her relationship with Shawn above God over the past few years.

"Whatever my butt. The next time you go to church will be at my wedding."

"Ha-Ha! Yall are silly!"

The giddy girls were filled with ecstatic happiness and as usual, finding humor while amongst themselves.

*****

What she thought would be a fabulous adventure where she would spend the day listening to *oohs* and *aahs* didn't quite turn out that way. Being told 'no' after zipping into a gown that put a big smile on her face was just as unbearable as standing in front of a sales consultant semi-naked.

"Emma what is the website address so I can pull up the information on my iPad?" Sidney asked, while lying across the bed of their hotel suite.

"Www.bmwnetwork.com"

When the sun sets, Atlanta nightlife can be a melting pot of fun. They were craving to solicit one of the best venues it had to offer. An unmatched choice of entertainment, BMW Network afforded guests a monthly red carpet like atmosphere which featured a stellar lineup of writers and their books, a live band, wine of the month, comedy, spoken word and an after-party where they can dance the night away.

"Does it give you a start time?"

"Ummm...I'm looking right now."

Sidney began browsing the website.

"Okay. It says it starts at seven o clock."

"Okay cool. Well let's start getting ready so we don't be rushing."

Emma walked across the room to grab her suitcase.

"Hannah. What's going on with you. You seem to be in deep thought. You alright?" Emma asked, after tossing her suitcase on the bed. Hannah was sitting quietly with her back against the headboard.

She answered her not a word.

Emma could differentiate that something was wrong. Hannah was her best friend since middle school and she knew her very well.

She sat next to her. Hannah was teary eyed.

Putting her arm around Hannah's shoulder, "Hey girly was wrong?" she asked, as she began to console her.

Hannah was on an emotional minefield; a meltdown. The stress of wedding planning coupled with Alex wanting her to sign a prenuptial agreement was ruining the joy of being engaged.

For the next several moments, she verbalized her displeasure about everything; tearful tantrums.

"Well girlie look here. I am going to be honest with you. You know I am your BFF and I will always keep it real right?"

Hannah nodded her head and blew her nose with the Kleenex.

"I do see and understand both of you all's take on the prenuptial agreement. However, as your best friend and also as an attorney, I actually think you all should get one as well."

Hannah appeared ambiguous.

"Now we don't have time for me to explain to you all the facets of it and why it's recommended but I will tell you this..."

Her assertions were brief and basic.

Sidney chimed in, "Yea Hannah it's not as bad as you think. Don't stress out about it. Hell whenever Shawn gets married, he's going to have her sign a prenup to."

"And you better believe whenever I get married, my husband's ass is going to be signing one his damn self," Sidney uttered in a buffoonish tone.

"Girl don't you be over here crying and stressing out over nothing. I want you to let loose. We plan to have fun tonight and enjoy ourselves."

"Ok Hannah?"

"Alrighty," she responded with a grin.

After hearing their valued opinions, her spirit was naturally lifted as she felt less troubled about those concerns. She was much better able to harness her emotions.

"Alright now girl, give me love."

They shared a warm-feminine hug.

"And tomorrow we going to go meet with Reco Chapple and see if he can design you a dress."

Reco Chapple is an American fashion designer, as seen on Bravo TV.

"And then after that we going to the 'Turn Me Loose' stage play you want to see and we still got Sunday to look around before we go to the game."

"Okay cool."

"Now get up and get sexy and sassy so we can be on time for the event."

Sunday Night

Lying down in his bed, Cole was mentally distressed; just partially tuned into the television, he closed his eyes.

"Dear Lord, I offer you this prayer, to help me with my current relationship situation. Please take away all the pain and hurt in my heart that I have for Jenna...And Lord, my hormones are raging uncontrollably and I am trying to hold on and be patient and wait on Jenna to be healed physically, mentally and emotionally."

His plea was very genuine.

"So Lord please give me the strength to never surrender to the temptations that come my way."

He paused his complaint; temporarily lost for words.

"Matter of fact, lead me not into temptations and guide me every day. Make this complicated relationship become uncomplicated."

"Thank you Lord, for hearing my prayer. Amen."

The posture of Cole's heart was extremely

humble.

Taking control of his comfort, Cole placed another pillow under his head for higher elevation. He was lying on his back, watching a close game between the Atlanta Hawks, his hometown team, and Memphis Grizzlies.

The arena horn sounded. It was now halftime.

He switched the channel over to CNN.

Uttering his unguarded soliloquy, "Oh fuck I don't want to hear shit about trump today!"

Even though he is Caucasian, he was extremely bothered by Donald Trump's racially insensitive viewpoints about Blacks, Mexicans, and Women. Cole was always compassionate towards all humans. He also had Black and Hispanic friends and acquaintances, and so was a significant portion of his 7000-member congregation.

Cole quickly flipped back over to TNT and began to watch the halftime show. The illumination from his phone caught his eye. It was on silent.

He received a text message.

[Alyssa…8:34 P.M.]~~~ I'm on my way. Are you still at home or did you already leave?

[Cole…8:34 P.M.]~~~I'm at home. I'm sending you an E-Key so you can unlock the door with your phone.

Kevo was an innovative app that enabled customers to unlock doors with their phones.

[Alyssa…8:34 P.M.]~~~Alrighty then.

[Cole…8:34 P.M.]~~~And don't let me down.

[Alyssa...8:35 P.M.]~~~Oh I won't. You will be very happy when I'm done.

After Kenny, Charles, and Shaq sympathetically delivered hearty statements regarding the death of Craig Sager, their colleague and popular sideline reporter, Ernie, the studio host, ushered them into another segment of the program where they gave their analysis on the game.

Midway through the fourth quarter, Atlanta Hawks began to pull away. Dennis Schroder, the point guard for the Hawks converted a fast break layup, they were now up by 9. Cole was full of cheer; in good spirits.

*****

It was long overdue. Although he was married and in love with Jenna, he needed to explore his sexual options. He hurled her onto his bed; face down ass hoisted; tipsy off Dom Perignon.

"Ewww Shiit," she uttered, as he shoved his sex muscle in from the rear. She was like his fantasy harlot, with an angel face. And had the body of a Nubian Goddess.

Cole parted her geni lips with deep hard thrusts as he was enraged with sexual energy.

"Ooooo yeaaa! Fuck me daddy!"

Cole took masterly control as he was pounding her geni ferociously; imposing his will on her.

"Ohhhh yes! Fuck me harder, harder!"

Laboring husky breaths, he was stroking her relentlessly, reveling the ecstasy of their forbidden fuck session; unaware that Jenna, and his in-laws just arrived home from their vacation.

"Yes! Fuck this pussy daddy!"

She had a dominating personality, and was sexually dominant, but cherished being fucked in submissive positions; doggystyle.

"Oh yes! Fuck me real good daddy!"

The garage door rose. Cole didn't hear it. He was distracted by his lustful pleasures and her abrasive language.

He was showing no mercy. Fucking the shit out of her. In his home, marriage bed; with an animalistic expression. The best sex is always with someone you shouldn't be fucking.

Cole had no morale conviction about this illicit affair. His sexual excitement peaked at new dangerous heights.

"Oh yes!! Un-hn, Yes! Fuck me!" she screamed. Her geni was aching with pleasure.

Cole was grimacing, growling, aggressively driving his hips towards her curvaceous-jello ass.

With uneven breaths, he glanced down at his waist line; white secretions smearing onto his disc, violently pumping her drenched-cum geni.

The bedroom door opened. It was Jenna, in her power wheelchair. She couldn't believe what she was seeing.

Cole jerked up. His heart skipped two beats. He was disoriented.

"So is this what you do when I am gone away from the house jellybean?"

His blood pressure was just as high as his morning erection.

Squinting his eyes, he looked her direction but his vision was fragmented. He was startled out of a bizarre dream.

"You normally up bright and early watching Mike and Mike, but now you want to lay in the bed all day." Jenna said trivially.

"Oh hey Boobie how was your trip?" he asked, wiping away the slobber from the corner of his mouth.

Natural daylight permeated the room.

"It was nice. A much-needed getaway."

"Well I am glad you enjoyed yourself."

"I did."

"What time is it?"

"It's almost ten." Jenna replied.

"Really?"

"Yea. That's why I was surprised you was still in the bed."

"So what time did you go to sleep?"

"To be honest with you I don't know. I just remember laying here watching the game last night."

"Wow you must've been real tired."

"I guess I was more tired than I thought."

Cole untangled himself from the covers.

"So where is Chelsea and Peggy?" he asked.

"Oh they are out in the front room. They going to rest here for a few hours they said before they hit the road back to Indianapolis."

"Oh okay cool. Well let me get down there and chat with them for a bit."

He rose to his feet and slid on his house shoes that were on the floor next to the bed.

"Uh-Un," Jenna rejected, re-actively putting up an arm block as he leaned down to kiss her.

In a jesting manner, "don't be trying to kiss me until you go brush your teeth."

"Oh so it's like that now?"

"Now? ...It's been like that since day one. I don't do stank breath."

"You right, you right," Cole said.

He grabbed his cell phone off the bed before walking towards the bathroom.

"Oh yea jellybean, when you get done brushing your teeth, can you get my bags and suitcase out of the trunk of the car."

"Of course baby. I'll get it out in a minute when I come out to the living room."

He smothered the bristles of his toothbrush with Colgate and dabbled it with water from the faucet.

As he brushed, he began to reflect about the

woman of his dream. Not the naughty one from last night's slumber, but the woman he made a vow to on a beautiful afternoon in the spring.

Cole gargled and swished Listerine around his mouth.

He picked up his phone and scanned it for missed calls and messages.

[Alyssa…10:21 P.M.]~~~I just finished. Your lapel mic and all the other mics are programmed to perfection.

Their tech-savvy media and production director, Cole asked her on last night to connect and test all the microphones with the new sound system they had imported.

[Cole…9:58 A.M.]~~~Thanks a bunch, I really appreciate it.

[Alyssa…9:59 A.M.]~~~No problem. ☺

[Cole…9:59 A.M.]~~~By the way, how is your sister in Seattle doing?

She was an alcoholic, and Cole had been in recent prayers for her to shake the spirit of alcoholism. He knew the emotional distresses that came with it, as he witnessed it amongst his own close relatives.

[Alyssa…10:00 A.M.]~~~She is going better. She's almost finished with her 12-step program.

[Cole…10:01 A.M.]~~~Well that's wonderful. I will continue to pray for her and you do the same. Ttyl.

Chapter EIGHT

After hearing both arguments from the Georgia State prosecutor and Emma, his defense attorney, they were asked to stand for sentence hearing.

There was an absence of noise in the courtroom, but emotions were present. Alex, with a nervous thrust transpiring throughout his body, was uttering a final silent prayer. And so was his father, who stood next to him with his fingers crossed; hoping on a favorable ruling for his son Austin.

Judge Thomas Wilcox delivered his statements followed by the imposed penalty.

"It is here by the judgment and sentence of the court that as to both counts one and two, the defendant be sentenced to two years with the possibility of parole in 180 days."

Realizing that her son's life was just turned upside down, his mother broke into tears sobbing loudly as he was immediately handcuffed and taken into custody. He was a high school All American cornerback, homecoming king, and honor student. And it was just several months ago where he was fielding interest from colleges all over the country including Ivy League schools. Weeks after signing a full ride scholarship to play football for the Notre Dame Fighting Irish, Austin attended a party in Atlanta while on spring break, which turned out to be a life altering decision. Where he thought he would be sleeping in a dorm room in South Bend Indiana, he is now headed to spend at least the next 180 days at the Burrus Correctional Facility in the state of Georgia.

Exiting the courtroom, Alex was in a war with his own pupils, as the salty solution was brimming around his sockets. Part of him was disappointed in God for allowing injustice to take place and another part of him was angry with himself. For some reason, Alex felt responsible for the situation his brother got his self into.

Patting him on the back, "It will be okay son," said Alex's father, as they proceeded in walking through the hallways of the government building. This burden was too much for him to carry. He was confident that the God he prayed to would ensure that fairness was exercised, but it wasn't, according to Alex. And he was beginning to question his own belief system.

Falling to his knees, he surrendered to the pain. He was physiologically scorned and couldn't help but to weep as the liquid spilled from his eyes, wetting his cheeks.

"Get up son," his father said, as he stooped down beside him.

Alex feared for his brother, knowing the dangers that come with being in prison on a daily basis.

His father pacified him for about another minute,

and he eventually mustered up enough strength to stand erect.

"You have to be strong son. We are going to get through this," he said, as he put his arms around Alex.

"Now let's go get a bite to eat before we head back to Nashville."

There was a sweet ambiance in the living room as they were all enamored with the 7lb, 3-ounce bundle of joy in Terrance "TJ" Ingram Jr.

Monica was five days removed from the hospital and was glad to be back in the comforts of her own home.

"Awww...him is so cute!" said Hannah, as she cradled him in her arm.

"Alex, it looks like your wife-to-be is overly excited about holding a baby. Are you going to give her what she wants?" Monica said, leaning back in her recliner.

"Yea okay," he responded so not seriously. He was more focused on the television as the NBA analysts were voicing their perspectives on how great another upcoming finals match would be between Golden State Warriors and Cleveland Cavaliers. Both teams loaded with superstars.

"Monica, Alex is not paying you any attention and neither am I" Hannah responded.

Looking into his eyes, "Hey there auntie baybeeeee." she said, stretching out her vowels, in a high-pitched tone, accompanied with an exaggerated smile. Emma was sitting beside her; hovering over Hannah's shoulder, with sparkle in her eyes.

"You my little baybeee...are you my little baybeee...yes, yoooou are!"

"He looks just like his daddy" Emma chimed in.

"Terrance can't deny him one bit."

Emma participated in showering him with love and affection as she began to massage his tiny feet.

"Aww look at he" Emma said cheesing, as he started wiggling and curling his toes.

He babbles.

"Yes. You likey your feet rubbed...you likey feet rubbed."

His sensory experience was clearly heightened.

"Yea him like that."

Emma was pressing her thumb in small circular motions on the bottom of his foot.

"Hey Alex have you spoken to your brother?" Monica asked.

"Yea I actually spoke with him yesterday."

"Ok. So how's he holding up?"

He has been incarcerated for some weeks now.

"Uhhhh. You know he's still trying to get adjusted. You know all this stuff is new to him."

"Well you know Terrance has a friend in there. Maybe they can connect with each other while he is in there, so he will have someone he can talk to."

"Oh really...yeah what's his name?"

"His name is David Grinstead. They call him Day-Day."

"How old is he?"

"He's like 31 or 32, somewhere around there."

"He's in there for drug possession and carrying a gun without a license. He's been in there for several years. But I know he gets out in another year or two."

"Okay cool. Yea let Terrance know and have him reach out. I think it will be good for him to befriend somebody while he in there for the next several months" Alex responded.

"Okay. I will definitely let him know when he gets home. He should be home any minute now."

"Oh and write down Austin's address for me so I can write him sometime and keep him encouraged."

She handed him a pen and an envelope. It was junk mail.

"Just write it on the back of this."

A little over an hour into their visit at Monica's, baby TJ fell asleep.

"Girl you be sure to call me if you need anything" Hannah said, as they all stood adjacent to the front door.

"Okay girl I will" Monica replied as she opened up the door for them.

"Alex I know you not going with them are you?"

"Girl no! He's not coming."

Hannah and Emma were going to shop around for wedding apparels.

"Okay well don't chew me out. I was just making sure. I know you are new to this."

"No girl I know better than that now. We are going drop him off at the car lot and then head out."

An astute business man, he was the owner of Victory Car Rental.

"Besides, he's too cheap anyway. He would get on my nerves."

They were extreme opposites. Alex was a not-quite-on-sale-enough kind of guy, and she had an expensive taste, especially for a dress that was the centerpiece of the most important day of her life.

Just before leaving, Emma, Sidney, and Alex each said their goodbyes and embraced her with a hug.

"Ya'll be careful!" Monica said, just as she closed the door behind them.

Above being known as one of the most notable Pastor's in Nashville, Cole was also regarded as a therapist for couples. The uniqueness of his sessions was the contrasting dialogues he fostered. Even though he was a religious clergyman; his observations were not exactly spoken within spiritual realms, but to some degree from secular measurements. He understood that many of the couples were not only unsaved or un-churched, but they did not even belong to his congregation even if they were Christians. His primary approach was to enrich and help all intimate situations, no matter their choice of lifestyle. And over the years, Cole has coached many partners through issues that seemed at first insurmountable by expressing to them fundamental truths where they can make decisions on, rather than reactive emotions.

"So Kevin. I want you to turn towards Tracy and tell her exactly what it is you want from her."

They were in his apartment office, his listed location under professional counseling. Because Kevin and Traci were members of Abundant Faith, coupled with him being their wedding officiate, it was a requirement for them to complete his *Before You Say I Do* course.

In a frustrated tone, "Mr. Cole, that doesn't even matter. It has to already be in you. I can't make her become what she is not."

Cole began twirling his thumbs; his facial

expression was unyielding.

"Kevin..."

There was a short pause. Kevin looked at him; uncompromisingly.

"The same way you are talking to me...you need to look over at Traci, and voice to her how you feel."

They were sitting on the loveseat that was a few feet in front of his custom glass top desk. His office was distinctively furnished; equipped with Crate&Barrel.

Kevin turned towards her, reluctantly.

"Baby. It's not that I want you to give me head. I want *you* to want to give me head."

Cole didn't mind his unfiltered language.

"Well um..." she said, shrugging her shoulders.

"When I feel like I can trust you, I may want-to-want-to give you head. But until then..."

Punctuating her defensive rebuttal, she crossed her legs dismissively; slightly turning away from him.

"See there!" he erupted, throwing his hands in the air.

"Kevin you can get mad all you want! I'm not gonna be sucking ya dick because I don't trust your ass!"

"Hey hey hey," Cole intervenes, trying to control the hostility.

"Now you see what I'm talking about Mr. Cole...Now you see!"

He gave them a moment of sound advice on fair fighting.

"Okay Traci" he said, after diffusing the tension between them.

Candid conversations and discussing combustive issues often stir up emotions.

"Explain to me why you don't trust Kevin."

"Because he cheated on me."

"Seven years ago" Kevin interrupted, raising a hand and a finger's deuce with the other.

She directed at him a boxer's stare. The kind at the weigh-in press conference.

"Anyways, as I was saying. He cheated on me. And just as recently as...a few months! ...ago."

Her voiced thickened.

"I went through his phone and saw text messages he was sending to some bitch. Not to mention all them hoes he flirts with on facebook."

"And there lies the problem I have with you. I've told you plenty of times to stay the fuck out of my shit" Kevin said. His frustration shoved sanity out of the window.

"Hey-hey!" Cole shouted, immediately suspending Kevin's toxic reaction.

"You have to stop attacking her with that level of tenacity and verbiage...never verbally assault her especially when she is vulnerable."

Written all over his face, Cole was clearly disappointed.

"Kevin you have to treat her sensitivities with care and try to listen to her when she conveys her thoughts and feelings."

"You understand?"

"Yes sir," he responded, as if Cole was his big brother and he was pledging a fraternity. Kevin was an Omega; earning his letters just over an hour away at Alabama A&M University.

"Healthy communication is key to sustaining relationships. And the only way you can have that is not only with openness and truth about your concerns, but in an environment of emotional safety…an environment where your partner can address to you their problem, and you listen...without yelling and hollering and being defensive. Because all of that will only prevent you from being close to your partner."

Cole glanced down at his trendy *TagHeuer* timepiece.

"Now with that being said, Traci you shouldn't go through his phone. That is his phone and everyone deserves some level of privacy."

"But if he isn't doing anything and have nothing to hide what difference does it make?" Traci questioned, moving away the hair strands from around her eye.

"Well it makes a difference for one, because he doesn't want you going through it. And you should respect his wishes. Secondly, unless you are willing to forgive him, you definitely shouldn't go through his phone. And thirdly, he may have private messages in his phone that's not for you to see."

She telegraphed her derision with a smirk, picking imaginary lint from her clothes.

"Like for instance. My wife doesn't go into my

phone or snoop around because I have people telling me things all the time that should remain confidential. Things that they trust me with as their Pastor or relationship counselor that they may not want my wife to know."

"But that's understandable because of who you are."

"No not necessarily. Kevin's mom or brother may text him a message that's private and personal for his eyes only, and if you snooping through his phone and see it, then there it goes...basically that's not right Traci. Unless he gives you permission then cool, but don't be snooping through his phone like an amateur detective. He deserves that level of privacy."

He peeked at his watch again.

"Lord time flies...we only have a few minutes remaining."

"So Kevin let me ask you this. Why do you engage in inappropriate conversations with women on facebook?"

"Ummmm," he said, mentally reflecting on his own behaviors. He had somewhat of a rugged personality; from the deep south; raised in a Louisiana impoverished neighborhood with abandoned homes and graffiti buildings, and a barrage of black boys without fathers. But at the core, he had a selfless love for Traci.

"I honestly don't think it is inappropriate. The conversations are more or less of me being overly cordial."

"So why are you overly cordial?"

Keeping her composure, Traci sat with a

condescending calmness.

"Well mainly because I am a performer; lead singer for a band as you know. And my songs and lyrics are about love and sex…so sometimes I may invite women out to my shows or what have you."

He was a gentleman with effortless charm and always gained favorable will from women.

"So what do you say when you invite them out?"

"Ummm…Hell I don't know…I just say whatever comes to mind like….um…"

He was lost for words. And Traci was now shifty. Twirling her fingers. Pressing her tongue against her teeth.

"Like I will compliment them or something like that, and just sort of spark up a nice warm conversation. Make them feel special because I know that's what they like."

Traci's emotions shuffled over to her bitter station. The audio content transmitting her ears was disturbing.

"You can't just simply invite them out without all the sweet talk?"

"I mean I guess I can. But...I get better results if I engage in conversation with them…because honestly, many of them end up buying my album or downloading it on iTunes…you know what I mean…but real talk, at the end of the day I don't care about them girls. I'm just trying to sell my brand and make money and I have told Traci that over and over again."

"Whatever Kevin," she said, making a stare at the couples-picture framed on his wall. It made all the sense in the world to Kevin, but to Traci his logic was just as believable as a dime-store psychic.

"But I will admit. I enjoy the company and conversations of various women and sometimes I may go a little bit too far with it…I'll admit that."

"Well I am glad you admitted it and recognize the wrong in it. Acknowledging the mistake is the first step and a fundamental tool in the arsenal of problem solving."

"Okay love birds, we have about three minutes left. I want both of you to write on your notepads these questions."

They removed the caps off their pens.

"This is you all's homework assignment I need you to complete before our next session. And don't share your answers or let the other see…so no snooping!"

"You got that Traci?" he asked frivolously.

"No more snooping of any kind."

"Yea I here ya," she responded, easing into a hand-me-down smile.

"Okay. I got three questions. The first question is…"

"Of all the persons you could have married, why are you choosing your partner."

They began writing the question down in their individual notepads.

"Okay. Your second question is..."

"What do you expect of a marital partner in terms of emotional support during exciting times, depression, and periods of illness or job loss."

Considering it was a lengthy question, he repeated it.

"What do you expect of a marital partner in terms of emotional support during exciting times, depression, and periods of illness or job loss."

They both eventually looked up at him, indicating they were finished.

"Alright. Now the last question is..."

"What rituals will you develop to reach out to your partner after a big fight."

It wasn't rainbows and roses. It seemed to serve as an alternative destination for them to yell and clash rather than at home. But after leaving the office, it was overall an effective session to Traci and Kevin. Cole taught them new approaches on how to deal with their issues. They were still unsure of how the course would benefit them in their future marriage, but they figured as long as they learned how to resolve conflicts amicably, and their relationship strengthened, it was worth the time and effort. In their heart of hearts, they deeply loved one another.

Chapter NINE

"You need anything before I go to the office to work?" Cole asked Jenna as she was lying in the bed, tucked under the covers. It was a few minutes after ten, in the middle of the night.

"I'm okay baby thanks."

"Okay goodnight. I love you."

"I love you too" Jenna responded, as Cole left the room.

Cole was incapable of staying on task from the start. He had writer's block; flipping through page after page in his NIV Bible. He prayed and brainstormed. And after a flash of brilliant ideas, he was able to piece together two enlightening sermons. One for the upcoming Sunday, and another for an approaching revival he was expected to preach at in Richmond, Virginia.

Jenna was fast asleep and snoring. But she jarred, involuntary, disturbing her own rest.

She rolled over and glanced at the clock on the nightstand. It was after midnight and Cole wasn't in the bed.

Is he still in the office working Jenna mentally reflected.

She stretched and yawned, and seated herself in the power wheelchair by the bed.

Jenna maneuvered around the sectional in the social room, to check up on Cole. Just as she approached the glass French doors of the office, she overheard him talking.

"Why don't you make it clap for me" his even-toned voice said, as he was in the heat of the moment.

Jenna crept. She was speculative.

She could now see him through the glass door. He had his hands in his pants; tapped into his primal nature.

"Damn that ass is amazing."

Jenna became angry. Her heart was beating like a bass drum in her chest. She was pinching the bridge of her nose, vacillating on what to do about her husband having cybersex. Her anger blended with understanding as a tear fell off of her face.

Latching on to her anguishing emotions, she calmed the best way she could, but still uttered a loud cry.

Cole was flabbergasted by the familiar weep. He turned around; his wife was teary-eyed.

"Oh shit!" he said. He was staggering; the oddity of the circumstance faltering his body coordination.

He pulled his self together; fastened his pants, and logged off the computer; shot out the office to console his wife.

Cole and Jenna opened up new pathways of communication as he marched into an emotional account of his leisure pursuits and why he watched porn. He was straightforward and sincere.

"Baby just hear me out...okay" Jenna said, after she composed herself. She couldn't stay mad at him; it wasn't in her fiber.

"Okay." he responded.

Realizing that Cole loved and cherished her unconditionally, she looked at both sides of the coin and the role that her physical and emotional well-being played in it.

She exhaled a deep breath.

"Now I know this may sound crazy to you...And honestly, it probably is a little crazy...And I actually may regret what I am about to say...but..."

Cole's heart dropped; her prefix implying a marriage debacle. And for a well-known esteemed Pastor, divorce wouldn't be ideal.

"If you find someone that you want to get your rocks off with, it's okay."

Cole looked cloudy in the face. What Jenna told him was contrary to his common-sense beliefs.

"It's going to take some time for me to get used to but..."

"No baby stop, stop, stop. Please don't talk like that" he earnestly appealed.

"No you stop!" Jenna exploited. Her emotions re-aroused.

"I can't do anything for you!"

She began to cry.

"I'm in a shit hole, stuck in this fucking wheelchair! ...My dreams are gone! ...I can't pursue a career in acting. I can't be a satisfying wife to my husband! ...I'm just all fucked up Cole!"

Jenna was sobbing. Cole became gushy himself by her grossly sentiments.

"No you're not baby!"

"Yes I am!" she screamed, as she pounded her fist on the arm bar of her chair.

"Stop pissing on my doorstep and telling me it's raining! ...You and I both know this marriage and everything is all fucked up! ...I know you're not totally happy because I am not totally happy! ...How can I make you happy if I am not happy!"

Jenna was realistic about issues and always had an offbeat personality. Even as a teenager, she regularly pushed boundaries and disobeyed family rules. She loved the notion of Cole's happiness more than hers and felt that giving him permission to cheat was a marriage saving arrangement. She understood that sex, especially for a young couple, was the underpinnings of companionship.

Dripping in tears, "Do whatever it is you have to do, but just don't leave me baby...That's all I ask."

As far as she was concerned, emotional infidelity was much worse than physical infidelity and her attitude for sex outside of marriage was aloof.

Cole was obviously ambiguous. And the hopeless image of his wife was haunting his already torn mind.

"Never that baby. I am not leaving you nor am I

having an affair...We are going to get through this…you hear me?" he said with a strong conviction. He was extravagantly tender.

They continued to sentimentally address unwelcoming parts of their lives, but not for long. They drifted off to sleep, exhausted from the emotional catastrophe.

It was an extremely sad day for Nashville. The outpouring of cries filled the sanctuary of New Horizons church as nearly four thousand, mostly dressed in black, said their *goodbyes* as they mourned the loss of a hometown hero and legend.

His college teammate and good friend, added to the emotional service as he gave his sentiments.

"Shawn was more than just a basketball player or even a friend. He was like the only brother I had," Anais Thompson said, rubbing the tears away from his eyes with the back of his hand. He played alongside of Shawn at Glencliff high school and they both shared the same back court at University of Kansas, leading their team to a fantastic season before losing in the championship game of the Final Four just a year ago.

As soon as he began to recall their past mutual experiences, he was disturbed by the loud shouts and weeps of Sidney. She wasn't prepared to meet these emotions. The pain was overwhelming and abundant.

What she initially thought was a prank of him playing dead was an actuality the sunrise of April 1st. It was customary for Crystal, Shawn's companion of two years, to salute him with breakfast every morning before basketball practice. After yelling 'your food is ready' a few times from the kitchen, Crystal presumed he was in a deep sleep and that he just didn't hear her. She then went to the bedroom to wake him by tapping Shawn on the shoulder. Shawn didn't respond. Instinctively, she believed it was one of his good nature antics. After all, it was April fool's day and Shawn was a habitual jokester. But after nudging him several hard times, her intuition kicked in. The love of her life was unresponsive and she immediately called emergency personnel. And it wasn't until later that afternoon, he was pronounced dead after suffering complications from sleep apnea.

Looking down at his lifeless body in the pearl white casket, "Shawn led by example. He was a natural leader," said his high school head coach, who spoke highly of his character. Staged on both ends of the casket were memorabilia; Glencliff football and basketball jerseys framed, as well as his Kansas Jayhawk jersey and his Memphis Grizzlies Jersey.

"I want my baby back!" Shawn's mother screamed at the top of her lungs. His family expressed their pain in tears, and the pitiful laments of Sidney and his mom ignited others to cry not only for the loss of the Nashville legend, but for their emotional health as well.

"He was full of life and love for others," his coach mentioned to the crowd whose hearts were shattered. This celebration of life included a photo slide show played on the large screen above the stage with images of Shawn's childhood, high school, college, and brief pro career. He was only a rookie. 21 years of age. Declared for the NBA draft after his sophomore season.

"So, how do we brace ourselves for the storms of grief?" Pastor Cole asked rhetorically, midway through his Eulogy. His counsel was very uplifting and nurturing to their souls.

Present were Shawn's current teammates, other NBA players and media representatives of the NBA. The funeral was aired live on ESPN2.

"How do we arm ourselves with tools to stay afloat, so we don't get lost in the torrential sea of grief we've been thrust into?"

Pastor Cole's laudatory speech of solace was immediately followed by a closing hymn, Precious Lord, by soloist *Je'Melody*, as the affluent walked around the altar to view his body one final time. But even in the midst of her beautifully delivering the song, the atmosphere grew disastrous. Emotions flared, and the sorrow was magnified. Sobbing relatives and close friends were fainting in grief around the coffin. Arguably, death via loss of a loved one is the most difficult valley a human can endure.

After about a two-hour service, the procession was held at Mount Olivet Cemetery for a private burial. The hearse, carrying Shawn's casket was escorted to the location by police officers on motorcycles along with several other vehicles transporting family members. The graveside service was punctuated with the releasing of white doves circling in the sky, enabling his closest loved ones to begin their process of letting go.

Friday Morning...

It was a quarter before 7 A.M. Cole was chowing down on his Renaissance Hotel room-service breakfast plate, while watching ESPN's Mike and Mike. But he was depleted, weary brained. Eyes bloodshot red. He betrayed his bedtime the night before. He was up til 3 A.M., watching porn, self-stimulating his sex organ during a web-cam session with Cherokee. Clergymen tend to let the demons out on the road. Cole was in Richmond Virginia, on a preaching assignment. He was the Thursday night speaker for the three-day revival at St. Paul Tabernacle.

His phone vibrated. It was a text message.

[Naomi...6:46 P.M.]~~**I'm finishing up the slides and fliers right now as we speak. Will bring by the church this afternoon. Will you be there?**

Cole emailed Naomi his sermon points and scriptures last night before heading to the revival service. He preferred to look over them prior to submitting to their audio/video engineer.

[Cole...6:47 P.M.]~~**Yes I will be there. My flight lands at 10:10. I'm going straight to the church from the airport.**

[Naomi...6:47 P.M.]~~**Ok see ya later.**

Opening up his facebook app, there was a litany of notifications. Mostly likes, and an array of comments stemming from his photo status of a large body of water overlapped with '*If God's grace was an ocean we would all be drowning.*' And there was a friend request from Shauntelle Carter, who lived in Richmond, Virginia. Black and Spanish, her entire face had traits of beauty, looking just like the vixens on the front cover of mainstream magazines. He suddenly remembered her. She appeared to be young and impressionable. She was the woman in the navy-blue polka dot dress sitting in the aisle seat at last night's revival. And there were about a dozen in-boxes, one from Katy Arnold, who had an unsavory reputation. It was a rather lengthy sexually charged message. She was the tramp that everyone knew joined Abundant Faith for all the wrong reasons. The next message came from Jessica O'Brien, in Murfreesboro, Tennessee. Her husband cheated on her and as far as she was concerned, she was ready to start enjoying life with various suitors herself; and Cole was the perfect candidate for revenge. And then there was a message from Michelle Baker, with the softball breasts and a shapely backside, who always dressed slightly above the line of inappropriate. Like a scripted piece of entertainment, her ass was so impressive that whenever she sashayed around the church for tithes and offerings the service came to a halt. The last message he opened was that of Vicky Adams; likened to supermodel Candice Swanepoel. She was relatively tall with long hair, high cheek bones, whose nine-year-old daughter was autistic. Her showstopper smiles at the brethren of the church are often misinterpreted as flirting by their wives.

Cole was just simply passing time. And more than enough had passed. After scrolling his news feed cluttered with TGIF posts, he put his phone away and gathered his luggage. The hotel shuttle bus was departing in less than 20 minutes to transport guests to the airport terminal.

*****

Friday 2:43 P.M.

"Hello Pastor," said the secretary, just as Cole walked in the main doors of the church. She was tuned into *Miss Kellis World* youtube channel on her phone.

"Hey there Yolanda" he said as he walked up to her. He was casually supporting his weight against the desk unit.

"So how was your flight?" she asked.

"It was great. I didn't do anything but sleep. I was tired. Your Pastor is always grinding; trying to lead by example."

"Yeah I can't take that from you. You always working hard."

In vitreous humor, "But I know who's not working hard," he said, staring in Gary's direction, the church custodian. He was spraying and wiping down the windows with a rag and bottle of Windex.

Gary overheard him. But he never turned around. He continued to clean.

"I know too. It's the young lady at the desk," he expressed comically.

"Ha Ha Ha...Mind ya business."

"Uh oh" Cole responded in a juvenile tone.

"Anyway Gary, do me a favor."

He turned around.

"What's that?"

"I have two appointments that intersect. I'm supposed to go get my car detailed in about 30 minutes, but I also have clients coming within an hour...So I need you to drop me off at the apartment office real quick and then take my car over to get cleaned."

"Okay no biggie. You ready to go now?"

"Yep I'm ready to roll."

A little over an hour later…

"Good afternoon," a gleeful Yolanda said to Naomi, as she walked inside of the building.

"Good afternoon, Yolanda!"

It was the weekend effect of Friday, when people experience better moods and greater vitality knowing they have additional freedom to choose their activities and spend time with loved ones.

Passing by the secretary's desk, Naomi walked down the hallway towards the offices.

She passed up her office and knocked on Cole's door.

She turned the knob to walk in, courtesy of his open-door policy. But the door was locked.

"Hey Yolanda has Pastor came in yet?" Naomi asked, after walking back to the front.

"Yea he was here a while ago. Gary dropped him off at the apartment office and then took his car to get washed. He said he had an appointment."

"Oh okay. I'll just drive over there."

Naomi got in her Nissan Altima and drove over to the church apartment office. Cole was expecting her anytime now. Not only was it the location for his professional counseling sessions, but it served as a convenient place to settle in between services on Sundays and Wednesdays, where he could take a nap, shower, and tidy up.

She pulled opened the glass door to the lobby of the complex. Trotting through the edgy lounge that featured game tables and a wine bar, Naomi pushed the elevator button and waited, with her designer tote bag drooping from her shoulder.

Using her key, she unlocked the door of unit 7046. Beyond the doorstep was plenty of square footage and panoramic views. Two bedrooms. In the master suite was a queen size bed, comfortable futon and a flat screen television. The second bedroom was converted into an office, where consultations took place. And adjacent to the gourmet kitchen was a spacious living room area where clients waited to be called into the converted bedroom-office.

After dropping her bag on the rectangular center table, she loitered around the kitchen and helped herself to a Fiji water and a sack of barbeque Grippos. Taking a seat on the bar stool, she snacked away.

“Okay Imani and Lamont. I want you all to jot down these questions before you depart from here. And when you come back next week, we will go over them. But don't let each other see your answers.”

They were a Christian couple, but not members of

his church. And even though they were there for counseling, Imani and Lamont weren't engaged or married. Just an ordinary couple. Fairly new. Seeking guidance on how to maintain a healthy relationship.

"Why do you love your partner?"

It was a routine assignment he asked of his clients. Just as he did Kevin and Traci.

In her spiral notebook, Imani began to write the question.

"I need a pen Mr. Cole" Lamont said, as he was fiddling through his pockets.

"Kuntry what happened to the pen I gave you earlier?" Imani asked.

Kuntry was the nickname she gave him. Not just because of his mannerisms, but for deeper issues.

"I think I forgot it in the car."

Cole tossed him one of the many ballpoint bic pens from his container.

Lamont removed the cap, and began to write.

Imani was finished. And quite frankly already knew her reasons. She had a herd of them. Lamont was completely unlike any other person she encountered. He birthed her a spiritual life, acquainting her with the Jesus that lived in him; Who saw her potential while in her predicament; treating her like a normal person but yet unconventionally; in manners unfamiliar to her conscience. In her secular life, normal was being born a crack baby. Normal was unshared emotions with her crackhead-prostitute mother. Normal was being molested by her uncle, cousin, and neighborhood mechanic. Normal was physical abuse by her grandmother who raised her not out of love but for financial gain. She was paid by the state. Normal was being hated by that same grandmother, because Imani's mother, had sex with grandma's boyfriend years ago. Normal for Imani was in and out of foster homes, all throughout childhood. She didn't graduate from high school. She ran away at 17, moved to Charlotte, North Carolina, and started stripping at Club Onyx, where married men, pimps and bachelors viewed her only in sexual conquest. That was normal for Imani. That's all she knew. Each of her experiences with men were sexual. They were sex demons and women were angelic sex slaves, at least from her perspective. So when she met Lamont she was drawn to him. He was fascinating. Winsome. Different; like a foreign country. That's why she calls him 'Kuntry'. He edified her. He was her first of many. The first to introduce her to his mom, who was the first to embrace her as a daughter. The first to tell her he was proud of her. The first to compliment her character. The first to invite her to church. The first to do her a goodwill favor. The first to touch her without actually touching her. And she was touched by it. She had a virgin blush. No carnal knowledge of a man that loved her unconditionally.

Lamont and Imani completed writing down all the questions asked of Cole. But before leaving, the three of them formed a circle holding hands, for a quick prayer.

Cole offered these words:

"Heavenly Father, as your worthy servant comes before you, we humble ourselves and prepare to listen to your word. In this union of love that Lamont and Imani have formed, I ask that you give both of them the patience needed to make this relationship a successful one. I ask that with you at the forefront of their lives, that this relationship becomes or remains pleasing to you, and that trust and faithfulness be ever present amongst this couple. And I ask that you remove the dark cloud that has passed over Imani's life, and to restore to her goodness, and by a miracle recover the love that is lost from people that should be close in her heart."

"Yes Lord" Imani uttered aloud.

"Remove her sadness and disappointments and give both of them the strength to resist the temptation and continue trying being a good mate for each other despite whatever challenges that come their way. And as they are led through this amazing life, put it in their hearts to love and trust you immensely. O God you have worked tremendous wonders to bring them together and we thank you for it. We attribute all the great things to you. So Lord, bless this relationship, as you have already done, and give them strength, hope, and love that keeps their hands outreached. But most importantly, help them to discover the roles and purpose you have for them. In Jesus name."

"Amen," they said in unison.

Cole walked them out of the office and escorted them through the front room where Naomi had just finished snacking away.

"You guys have a good day! See you in two weeks."

"Well hello there Naomi!" he said, after closing the front door.

"Hey, hey, hey!" she responded skittishly.

"How long have you been sitting out here?"

"Oh not that long. Only about ten minutes or so."

Feigning her disappointment, "I have a bone to pick with you."

"Oh lawd. Well that ain't nothing new."

"So tell me, what did I do this time?"

"You had me drive allllll the way over to the church and you weren't there."

It was such a bland account.

"Oh my bad. I'm sorry you had to drive a whole extra two miles back over here" Cole stated, in a sarcastic tone.

Naomi rolled her eyes; a counterfeit expression. She sipped from her bottled water.

Cole chuckled; titled his head to the side; hands on his hips.

"Why you so cray cray?" he asked, further engaging in their playful attitudes towards each other.

Fiddling with the metal clip in her hair, she lowered her chin, "Because you drive me cray-cray."

He just stood there. Hands still on his hips; non-threatening; staring at her.

"Girl I tell ya, you something else."

Naomi was a piece of work. Like a difficult puzzle.

Conventional with an edginess to her. She was the kind of girl that expected a man to open the door for her, but dared him to slap her on the butt when she walked by.

"Cray Cray come back here and show me what you got," he said, as he treaded back towards the rooms.

Naomi grabbed her miniature Gucci purse and bottled water off the counter. She picked up her tote bag from the center table and proceeded behind him.

"You know Alicia and Robert are getting a divorce, right?" Cole mentioned, just as she stepped into the room.

Naomi put her purse on the bed and sat down on the futon.

"Who's that?" she asked, pulling her laptop from the bag and placed it on the futon beside her.

You remember...the man with the glass eye that used to go to our church...he divorced his wife to go marry his mistress."

Cole scooted the accent chair over next to her so he could see the screen on her laptop.

"Oh yea I remember him..."

"But my goodness didn't they just get married not long ago?"

"Yea last October...They was upset that I wouldn't officiate the ceremony, so that's why they stopped coming to church" Cole said, as he sat down sideways in the chair; informally, facing her direction with his leg propped over the arm rest.

"Oh yea I don't blame you. Nobody wants to get

involved with that foolishness."

She hit the power button on her MacBook Pro laptop.

"Exactly...I'm glad they left. You raising hell in the church annnnnd, you not tithing."

"Ha!"

"So why they divorcing?" Naomi asked.

"He was cheating on her."

"Hell what do you expect. You marry the man that was cheating on his wife with you. Of course he's probably going to cheat on you too" Naomi said.

"But the killer part is, he was cheating on her with his ex-wife."

"O my God I've heard it all...you leave your wife to marry your mistress. But yet you cheat on your mistress with your wife."

Cole shook his head in disbelief.

They went into a deep discussion about daily functions, operating budgets and ideas on building an interactive website for the church. Cole highly valued her opinions. She had a flowery imagination. She was smart; a child prodigy, and graduated top 5% from the prestigious Emory University in Atlanta. This portion of their meeting lasted a long while, before hunger kicked in. They ordered Chilis-To-Go and satisfied their appetites. Then they got back to work. Addressing finances, advertising campaigns, and marketing strategies for this summer's vacation bible school.

Cole got out of the chair and sat next to Naomi on the futon. They were finally going over the slides she created for his Sunday sermon.

"You got them mixed up. Put hypothesis *B* where *A* is, and *A* where *C* is," he stated, pointing at her mistake.

"Cole if you don't stop touching my computer screen with your greasy hands we are going to fight."

He had just finished eating chicken wings and fries.

"Whatever. If you would've just put it together in the correct order the first time, I wouldn't have to touch your screen."

She paused. Gave him a menacing stare; but couldn't resist a half smile. It was a lingering smile that felt like an abomination to Cole.

Naomi made the corrections, but not before gulping a few swallows of her glass filled Pinot Noire. The same wine they serve on communion Sunday; Cole keeps bottles at the penthouse office.

All business matters were complete. Cole and Naomi dallied around the room on opposite ends of the futon, exchanging laughs, smiles, and butterfly babbles. Crossbreeding sips of wine with trifling topics, Naomi began moving in ways designated to catch his eye. And when Cole articulated his ambitions, Naomi was smitten, shifting closer. And after several subtle shifts throughout their progressing conversation, their legs were touching.

Grabbing his fingertips, "Cole why do you bite your nails so much?" she asked, with sparkles in her eyes.

"Ummm. I don't know. It's a habit I've always had."

Naomi drank the last bit of wine in her glass and sat it on the floor.

She leaned in closer to him.

Because of their long-standing friendship, they were always very comfortable in each other's space.

"Well don't you think you need to break that habit...Your nails are extremely short" she said, as she started to play with her hair. It was long and straight with honey blonde streaks.

"I've tried stopping before, but I always end up biting them again...I normally nibble on them when I am thinking and preparing my sermons."

"That's a nervous habit...are you nervous?" she questioned, as she lightly rested her hand on his thigh. She could really care less of his reasoning. And Cole discerned it as well. Naomi just wanted him to know he had clearance for go-ahead maneuvers.

"No I wouldn't say I am nervous. It's just something that I do that's all."

"Oh okay," she replied as she looked at him as a handsome cavalier.

Naomi adjusted her dress up top that didn't need adjusting; bringing attention to her bosomy breasts.

She continued asking him questions, soft soaping him, cajoling him with feminine chants.

"You want some more wine?" she asked, when she noticed his glass was empty.

"Yea that's fine."

She stood up from the futon and strutted over to the short espresso table across the room; leaning over further than necessary. She was wearing a knee length summer dress and what she like to call her Betty Wright classic pumps; a musical artist, with a popular song titled *No Pain No Gain*. These were the kind of heels that ached her feet but was a sexy distraction.

Naomi poured his glass three quarters full. It was a stemless 18-ounce. She never minded catering to a man because she was accustomed to it. She had a turbulent childhood. Her mom passed away when she was a baby, and being raised by a single father, she saw firsthand the challenges of a man without a female companion and having to undertake roles that are typically assumed by a woman. So when she was an adolescent, Naomi started to cook, clean, iron clothes, and naturally became attentive to her father's needs.

Meanwhile, back at the church...

"It's a blessed day in the Lord here at Abundant Faith; how may I direct your call?" Yolanda, the receptionist said.

"Hello Sister Yolanda how are you?"

"Hey First-Lady! I am fine. How's everything with you?"

"Aww. I'm hanging in there. Just keep praying for me."

"I sure will!"

"Thank you. But I don't want to hold you long. Is my husband there?" Jenna asked.

"Actually he's not. He's down the street at the office meeting with some clients."

"Oh okay. That's probably why he's not answering his phone...well can you leave him a message for me?"

"Sure!"

"Let him know that I'm in a different room now and to call this number when he can. I don't get good reception here in this building on my cell phone."

"Okay no problem Jenna I understand. What's the number?"

"It's 312-238-1000...Room 339."

"Okay got it. I will be sure to let him know."

Jenna was out of town at the Rehab Institute of Chicago. The #1 facility in the country that specializes in treatments of spinal cord and traumatic brain injury.

Naomi handed Cole the glass of wine and sat unethically close to him, crossing her legs. They were chatty and convivial. And as he sipped the wine, Naomi sweet-talked him; flattered him. And Cole sipped on, and she wheedled and wheedled. And he sipped. And she lured him, with beguiling words, insinuating to him take-me-now gestures.

Full of trivial conversations, they were merry and Cole's sips became gulps, like a nervous reflex. He couldn't control his libido. He had no defense against her sex appeal. Naomi had indecent thoughts, and knew Cole's body was screaming for intimacy. She wanted him to follow his personal desires rather than the rules of conduct. They were a conflict of interest; spiritually and corporately. He was a married man and her boss. And Cole himself was hesitant about her unspoken proposition.

Several naughty thoughts later, Naomi flashed him, like drunken girls on New Orleans's Bourbon Street. He didn't know how to proceed. It was one of the most bizarre situations he ever been in. Cole was somewhat socially impaired. Not by the wine consumption, but by aphrodisia. The perfect view of carnality momentarily blanked his mind.

Naomi lightly grasped him by the forearms, forcing his unholy hands to cup her breasts. Her nipples erect. His heart palpitating, palms sweaty. And the *WWJD* (What Would Jesus Do) bracelet on his wrist didn't sting his conscious enough to pull away.

She cradled her hand behind his head, drawing him closer to her. Face to face. Feverish breath. Greeting at the lips, they exchanged DNA samples along with their morals for self-satisfaction.

Cole came to his feet and removed his shirt and pants. He dropped his drawers freely to the delight of her talented fingers. And Naomi was impressed by his suit, just as she was with all his tailor-made suits. This was her first time seeing this suit. His birthday suit. It was tailor made, just for her.

Sitting on the futon, she secured his elongated disc, and groped; touching him where he had not been touched in quite some time.

Her head tilts backwards. She gave him a hasty stare, as she placed his crown on her raised chin; he was set apart for a particular task.

She teased him; Cole was under satanic agitation, feeling like God was allowing the devil to tempt him beyond his ability to flee from sin.

She glossed the king's crown; a metallic finish; tracing it across her luscious lips like a cosmetic liner.

Naomi rolled her neck and tucked a strand of hair behind her ear.

She took him in her mouth; he shrilled a manly moan; a physiological reaction, his body went into shock. He was seduced; unconcerned that their forbidden romance crossed over into dangerous territories.

She licked precum from his cock, and sucked. And the way she sucked reminded him of the first blowjob he received back in high school at Woodward Academy. A private institution. Mrs. Larson, she blew his brains out. She was a sassy brunette; his geometry teacher who had a fancy for conservative adolescents; handsome and distinguished; goody-two-shoes. And Cole had a sweet innocent quality about him. Cajoling him into transgressions turned her on.

"Ohhhhhhh-Shit!" Cole expressed. Naomi had the 'gift of tongues' and so did he, speaking in unknown languages; he didn't normally use profanity. But her powerful techniques caused him to utter words only understood by his sex God.

She gags. Catching her breath.

"Turn around" Cole said.

Naomi complied. She rested her upper torso over the futon cushion. Antsy just for appreciation sex, because she appreciated him; as a trusted friend. And she knew their cohesion would go no deeper than the six and a quarter inches he was about to give her.

Cole grounded at the knees, aligning his pelvis with her backside. He bunched her skirt at the back. Her ass out. She had a tramp stamp; abstract design between her dimple piercings.

He slid over her G-string and went in. Slowly. Her geni was abundantly wet. Mouth open, no words. She screamed a silent scream.

He pulled back. Slightly. And went in deeper.

"Ewww" she let out a kittenish moan. Cole was in a state of erotic consciousness as Naomi resurrected his once dead sex life.

"Oh yes!" she said, as Cole repetitively thrust.

Jenna was out of sight out of mind, as he created a false bond of intimacy, abusing his soul with sinful woes.

He heightened his stroke rhythm, abandoning himself to his deepest sexual desires.

"Oh-Oh-Ohhhh Yes! You feel so good! Give it to me!"

Cole stroking and grunting. Thrusting and sighing. Blessing her with his blessing; the type of blessing that brought tears to Naomi.

"Ewww-Yes!..Eh...Ah!..Ahhh!...Ahh!...Eh!"

Her groans grew louder. He was hitting her G-Spot. Pumping her geni doggystyle. And the louder she groaned, the more amplified the pleasure.

"Oh-Ah-Ah-Eh!"

Frozen in his tracks, Gary heard them, from the other side of the bedroom door. He had just returned from the car wash that Cole asked him to go to earlier as a favor.

"Ewww! Ahh!"

Cole heavily sighing and groaning. Naomi moaning. And Gary was snickering; incognizant of identical sins pleasing each other; he was eavesdropping on marital fidelity orgasmic moans. Four-part harmony; like a pop rock group. Maroon 5. Her alto *ewws* and soprano *aahs* in unison with his baritone *aahs.*

Gary only listened for a hot second. He left and drove back over to the church.

*****

"Hey Gary, I see you got Pastor's car looking all clean. You been out joy riding haven't you?" Yolanda asked, just as he was coming in.

He was grinning from ear to ear. She assumed it was a reaction to her presumption.

"No not necessarily. But had I known he wasn't going to be ready when I returned I would've stopped and ran a few errands while I was out."

Gary planted his elbows on the desk where Yolanda sat.

"So what time do you have to pick him up?" she asked.

"I'm not sure."

"So he didn't tell you a time to come back to get him?"

"No. When I dropped him off at the office, he just told me to go get the car wash and to pick up his suit from the cleaners and come back. So that's what I did. But when I got back he wasn't ready because him and First-Lady was being fruitful," he said with a huge grin.

Yolanda had a dumbfounded expression. It was very brief.

Forming a smile, "Whatever Gary I am not getting ready to play with you today!" she said, followed with a few chuckles.

"I'm serious. I swear to God I would not lie to you."

"Whatever Gary. You always playing," she said pleasurably.

"Look here. All jokes aside. Why do you think I came back after I stopped by the office?" he asked, trying to convince to her his truthfulness.

"I don't know why you came back. Maybe he was still meeting with clients."

"Look here. I'm telling you Yolanda."

He grabbed the bible that was on the desk.

"I put my right hand on this bible. And I swear for God that Pastor and First-Lady was getting it in."

She somewhat believed Gary as she looked at him with a small degree of belief, but she still couldn't totally accept it.

Yolanda suddenly remembered...

Drawing her lips back, "you want me to tell you how I know you lying?"

In a defensive tone, "I'm not lying Yolanda I swear to God. Do you actually think I would make something up like that right here in church and put my right hand on the bible?"

"No. You can say what you want. I just spoke with First-Lady not long ago. She called here from the rehab center in Chicago and asked me to leave a message with Cole."

Yolanda picked up the sticky note she wrote the rehab center number on and handed it to him.

"That's the number she called from and the room number she is in...Plus, its right here on the caller ID."

"Okay well. I know one damn thing. There are two people at that office" Gary said in a finite tone.

"Okay. That don't mean they having sex Gary."

"Yolanda. I'm telling you. I know what I heard. It was very clear what was going on in that room."

"Well if you heard two people in there having sex, why didn't you go in there to see what was going on?"

"Because I assumed it was Pastor and his wife!...I wasn't about to walk in on that. Which is why I left and came back here to the church."

"But it wasn't his wife Gary! I just spoke to her on the phone!"

"Well I know one thing. This is fact. There are two people at the office getting it in."

"Well who is it then Gary. Because I also know one thing that is fact. First-Lady Jenna is in Chicago" Yolanda said.

"Well let's add it up then. I dropped Pastor off at the office. And I have his car. You say First-Lady is in Chicago. So either A, Pastor is not at the office and decided to walk somewhere. And if he is not at the office, it could only be one other person there at the office. I have a key, you have a key, he has a key, and Naomi has a key. And if Pastor isn't there, and I'm obviously not there; you obviously not there, and Naomi not there, then that means somebody broke in and decided to do the-do and we need to call 911."

"Well Naomi stopped by here earlier for a quick second looking for Pastor and I told her he was down at the office. So she left and said she was going to go meet him there. So that means if she is still there and Pastor is there..."

She couldn't finish her statement. They both stared at each other, mentally articulating Cole and Naomi's guilt.

Putting her hand over her mouth, Yolanda was in awe. She couldn't cover her enormous grin. She burst into laughter along with Gary. The notion of their affair was laughable at the moment. And considering obvious circumstances, his dark secret was already beginning to lurk just beneath the surface of his unblemished image.

*****

An innocent meeting evolved into a mid-afternoon tryst. Not long after Naomi left, a teary-eyed Cole was lying on the floor face down.

"Lord please forgive me Lord" he expressed, kicking his legs like a newborn toddler.

It's puzzling how the flesh gets real strong after its been gratified. Cole couldn't believe what he had just done. Even though his wife gave him permission to cheat, the guilt and shame he harbored was overwhelming.

"Forgive me Lord God. Forgive me Lord God. Oh have mercy on me Lord Jesus."

Cole was at his lowest depths of despair; wanting forgiveness and to be cleansed from violating the seventh commandment.

"Lord Jesus I am so sorry. Please Lord forgive me," he begged. His heart was aching. His soul was shattered. He was regrettably sorry for his actions.

"Lord please, forgive me Lord. Please!... Stop by and see about me Jesus. Help me Lord. Forgive me Lord."

He was very contrite; crying tears of sorrow; suffering from his self-inflictions. And even though he cheated, monogamy was natural for him.

The pain was intense.

"Lord I don't know what to do. I need you right now Lord."

He was a conflicted man of faith, realizing the toxic triangle he created could explode or alter the course of his bright future.

He cried and sobbed. Runny nose.

"I feel so bad Lord. I feel so filthy Lord. I feel worthless Lord. Please forgive me. Without your forgiveness, I am nothing. But with your forgiveness I am whole again."

He lied there on the floor. Indefinitely; crying himself to sleep.

Chapter TEN

It was a night to remember that started on the Sabbath Day around 4pm, where over 600 guests, dressed in their upscale attire scrambled into the multi-story Omni Hotel. Themed peach and crème, immediately noticeable in the legends ballroom was a decorated arch at the forefront of the room and a custom white aisle runner engraved with cursive letters *A & H*, evenly splitting the rows of chairs with ivory covers with peach sashes.

After signing their names in the guest book, they took a seat on either the Stone or Carr side of the ballroom. The atmosphere was influenced by soothing romantic melodies of the talented pianist and saxophonist as the joyful parishioners mingled around and browsed through the program.

Suddenly, the lights slightly dimmed and all eyes transitioned towards the east corridor. Clarence McClendon, Alex's friend and Pastor of New Horizons began walking at a moderate pace in his all black tuxedo before standing underneath the arch. And immediately after came Alex, sporting a single-breasted suit and fancy wristwatch; he stood on the right side of the arch. Proceeding was Mr. and Mrs. Stone, being escorted down the center aisle by the usher to the first row followed by another usher escorting Mrs. Carr as well. The photographer snapped about a half dozen pics.

The beam of the lights diminished even more; heavily lacking in sharpness, but the ushers were providing artificial illumination, lighting the arranged candles around the ballroom. Accompanying them was the saxophonist composing subdued sounds idealized for the purity of the affair.

Slowly pacing their selves down the runner was Jalon, serving as the best man, and Emma, the maid of honor; clutched at the elbows, both smiling triumphantly. Emma was enraptured in both the moment but as well as the reality that the wedding planning was finally over. It was much more mentally taxing than she initially thought. At the end of the aisle, they unlocked and stood on their respective sides of the arch.

Everyone turned around in their chairs, looking back at the subsequent couple; Sidney and Harper, a friend of Alex that once tried to get at her. They had instant attractions but the interest wasn't lasting. Advancing slowly down the runner like megastar mates on Hollywood's red carpet, they looked absolutely fabulous. And there was a noticeable difference in Sidney. Aside from the additional pounds she was carrying from heavily drinking to escape the grief of her brother's death, coupled with frequenting restaurants with combo numbers, she was wearing a captivating smile that manifested from within. It was her aura. She apparently regained emotional stability. Just over six months ago she heard a sermon I MADE IT ON BROKEN PIECES by *Bishop Charles H. McClain*, and it was then where she felt revived and rededicated her life to Christ.

The final pair was equally impressive as they

came into everyone's sight, but were showing little emotion. Patrick, the cousin of Alex had worked all night prior and drove down to Nashville from Detroit that morning when he got off. And Monica, smiling fake smiles was just as lethargic. After walking the full length, they untangled themselves and parted ways.

Everyone was oohing and awing by the presence of the precious toddlers as their preciousness ignited the guests to smile. Baby TJ was now two years old, taking miniature steps as he carried the pillow with the ring tied to it. And nearby was his twin, 32 years his senior, his father Terrance, monitoring TJ's steps according to the role of ring bearer. And preceding TJ were darling duos with rosy cheeks; free of anxiety, toting their small peach baskets as they scattered rose pedals down the bridal path.

"Will everyone please stand for the entrance of the bride," said Pastor McClendon.

All persons stood to their feet and turned around as Austin began to sing Ribbon in The Sky in tune with the pianist. After his release from prison, he walked on at Vanderbilt University to play football, eventually earning himself a full ride scholarship.

The ushers opened the double doors; all eyes narrowed in on the woman in the white dress. She had a flood of unexpected emotions; erratic nerves, trying to embrace an ordinary life as a math teacher becoming a romantic fairytale. In her arithmetic dream of love, one plus one equals everything, and two minus one equals nothing. And she didn't even fall asleep last night because the reality was finally better than her dreams.

Her hair was pulled back from her splendid face; a

sophisticated bun at the nape of her neck, styled by *Mecai Adeola* in Studio City, California. Her father was standing next to her, just as nervous and apprehensive about giving her away. It was only a matter of minutes before his daughter would no longer carry his last name.

Making a grand entrance, Hannah advanced down the aisle alongside Mr. Carr in a luxurious mermaid gown with silk tulle from knee to floor, clutching a bouquet of lilies. She looked spectacular; her face covered with a huge dazzling smile, but the 101 smiles of her heart were even greater.

She met her groom under an altar filled with hydrangea, roses, and mini calla lilies in their wedding colors of peach and cream. Alex was smiling broadly, convinced he had accomplished something amazing, and Hannah was smiling because she was able to convince him of it.

Pastor Clarence McClendon gave his opening statement.

"Good evening, welcome to this most important moment in the lives of this couple as we invite you to leave behind the worries and concerns of everyday life and join us in the celebration of their marriage."

There was a substantial number of guests snapping pics with their cell phones.

"Our bride and groom have chosen this setting in which to be married because it provides an appropriate backdrop for the public affirmation of their love."

Heavily gazing into each other's eyes, Hannah and Alex reminisced about the moment they realized they wanted to spend the rest of their lives with each other, and how they wanted that moment to start as soon as possible.

"Hannah and Alex, your breathless tale is about to begin," Pastor McClendon stated.

"All you have to do is simply love one another and that love shows through in everything you do for one another, how you treat each other, in good times and bad."

McClendon's statement was followed by Hannah and Alex exchanging their beautifully expressed vows and rings.

After Alex presented Hannah with a Halo diamond ring, McClendon delivered his final announcement.

"Throughout this ceremony, Hannah and Alex have vowed, in our presence, to be loyal and loving towards each other...they have formalized the existence of the bond between them with words spoken and with the giving and receiving of the rings...therefore, it is my pleasure to now pronounce them husband and wife."

"You may now kiss your bride."

Alex, lifted the veil from her face and greeted his wife with a passionate kiss; there was an ovation of cheers.

*****

Following the nuptials, a reception was held down the hall in the Broadway ballroom, where tables were adorned with nude sequin linens and beautiful white centerpieces composed of lush roses and white orchids. And in the northeast corner was an amazing 5 tier strawberry cheesecake by *Cretia Cakes* of Indianapolis Indiana.

There was cocktail kickoff at the reception as guests waited on the newlyweds to finish posing for photos in the ballroom where the ceremony took place. The social milieu was enhanced by the band playing subdued conversation-friendly background music. But it wasn't long before they were alerted by the emcee of their imminent arrival; Hannah and Alex were introduced as husband and wife.

They entered into a roar of applause and then stepped into the spotlight; two souls with a single thought, two hearts beating as one, performing their first dance in unison with the live band as well as their 'Story of Us' slide show on the big screen. Hannah had changed into a more comfortable but gorgeous Badgley-Mischka dress with a crystal neckline.

The reception transitioned into an introduction of the wedding party, each verbally expressing their blessings towards the marital bliss, and then a tasty toast, followed by a celebratory meal. The dinner menu included organic pork chops, fresh fish, and beet salads. For dessert, alcohol-infused palates and ice cream was served.

The high emotions spread amongst the affluent as most of the giddy guests were taking improvised steps on the dance floor. Present for the event was also Cole, who was sitting at the tall oval table alone. He was a friend of Monica, one of Hannah's bridesmaids. Monica and her husband were also members of his church; and his ministry fellowshipped with Pastor McClendon's church quite often.

“Attention, Attention!” said Monica over the

microphone.

The rambunctious crowd lowered their voices.

"Will all the virgins please take a stand for the bouquet toss."

There was a slew of murmurs in the crowd as a wealth of invitees gave her an odd stare. Not one followed suit or got out of their chair.

The room was quiet.

In a defensive tone, "What! ...If you are not married wouldn't you be a virgin?" she asked. She couldn't hold back her grin.

Everyone pleasantly laughed as they intellectually grasped her silly request.

The bouquet toss somewhat defines the type of woman you are from an outsider's perspective. Bitter and standoffish women stand in the back, but join in to appease the bride; Jovial women that are desperate shove their way to the front; the ones in the middle are camera whores who want to be seen; The women standing on the side are content with just getting dicked down from time to time for right now. And the woman who catches it is the superficial and gossipy girl; the kind of girl that if a man slept with her, all her closest peers would know how big or small his package is.

With a winning smile, Hannah stood with her back facing the bachelorettes. The DJ blared up the music; Beyonce's *Put A Ring On It.*

After a count to three, Hannah threw it back over her head. It was snagged by Emma, who lunged for it like a life jacket on a sinking ship; the good spirited ladies shouted like a squad of cheerleaders whose basketball team just hit the game winning shot. Superstition is that because Emma caught it, she would be the one to share in Hannah's good fortunes and marry next. And rather it was true or not, she felt some type of way about it; especially since Jalon asked her earlier before they walked down the aisle why she wasn't married considering she was in her 30s.

The atmosphere was ripe with delight and tension. Watching from afar was Cole, sipping on one of the signature drinks. But out of the corner of his eyes he was distracted by the woman gaiting into the ballroom; heels clicking against the floor.

She staged her purse on the table; Kate Spade.

"I hope you don't mind if I stand over here with you," she said to Cole.

"Oh no, not at all. You're okay," Cole responded in a welcoming manner.

"So are you a guest of the bride or groom?"

"Actually, no in particular one. I know both of them. And Monica, one of the bridesmaids, is a member of my church."

"And what about you? Are you here on behalf of the bride or groom?" Cole asked.

"Neither."

"So who are you a guest of?"

"Besides this hotel I am staying in, I am not a guest of anyone."

Cole seemed to be confused, scrunching his nose and forehead.

"So who are you here for?"

She licked her lips; layered with a sheer of lip gloss. Commenced into his personal space; she straightened the knot of his necktie; he was well clothed; well groomed. And for any woman, a stylish dressed man is always the icebreaker for at least a conversation.

"I'm here for you," she candidly stated.

He chuckled nervously; he was thrown off by her indiscreet remark.

Finger drumming the table, he took a small taste of his wine and lowered the glass.

"So what is your name?" Cole asked, looking straight ahead. He was trying not to draw attention to himself. He was concerned about becoming the subject of Nashville gossip and media tabloids.

"Karmen."

"So what is your profession Karmen?" he asked, as he continued to avert his eyes away from her. But in his peripheral vision, he saw that she possessed characteristics more common to those of Cuban descent. Her hair was long and curly, flowing down her back. And her dialect and word pronunciation was atypical.

"I'm a Senior Finance Accountant for Ikea."

"Cool...I've been in your store a few times."

"You've probably visited one of our stores, but I doubt if you have been in my exact store."

"I thought it was only one location here in Nashville?"

"And you are correct. However, I do not work or live here in Nashville. In fact, I don't live here in the United States. I work out of the Dominican Republic."

He finally made eye contact with her. He was very perceptive. She had a distinctive tiny mole above her lips; like a young Cindy Crawford.

"So what brings you here to the States?"

"I'm here for work. I leave back out tomorrow afternoon. I've been here since Wednesday."

Cole began to rub the part of his neck below his earlobe; he was in deep thought.

"Isn't that a Spanish speaking country?"

"Yes it is."

"Soooo...are you bilingual?"

"Si, soy" she responded, standing unrestrained.

Cole laughed moderately; he was amused, but more intrigued by her casualness.

"Are you from the States?"

A woman across the ballroom observed Cole and the woman conversing. It was Sophia. She was a member of his church.

"Yes I'm from San Diego, California...graduated from San Diego State. After college, moved to Oregon and started working for Nike. I was bored; didn't really like it there. So I applied at Ikea and had to move to Portland. I got bored and established residence in West Hampton, New Jersey. Figured I'd like the east coast. But I didn't. I got bored again, and relocated my job to Houston. And then..."

"Let me guess" Cole interrupted.

"You got bored again."

She half-smiled.

"Yep I did. You must be a prophet" she said sarcastically; curving lips.

She continued with her assertions.

"Sooooooo, I left Houston and transferred to Dominican Republic."

"Oh wow. Out of the country I see."

"Yep."

"And when did you learn Espanol?"

"Oh I learned Spanish when I was a child. My mom is half white and half Cuban. And the town in San Diego where I grew up had a lot of Spanish speaking people."

Cole started stroking his chin; preoccupied; rationalizing.

Intensifying his voice, "so you are really not here for the wedding huh?"

"Mr. Whatever-your-name-is, I see you are very inquisitive. But I don't have any false pretenses. I was very direct when I told you I came here for you. Now do you want my company or do you not?"

Deterring her aggression, "Oh it's all good. I don't mind you being here. I'm just saying. It's not every day that someone will just randomly show up at a wedding. The last time I saw that happen was in the movie Wedding Crashers."

"I understand. But I'm not your average female. I operate out of the norm. I was bored out of my freakin mind and..."

Cole laughed.

"Oh my gosh. Don't tell me you were bored again" he said.

"Yep. So I came downstairs to have a drink in the lobby. That's when I saw the hostess, and wedding coordinator mounting up signs by the door. And I figured it wouldn't be a bad idea for me to chime in on the ceremony to pass time.

"So you just came on in huh?" Cole stated. He was intrigued by her consciousness.

"Yep. Just something to do. So I got dressed and came in and sat a few rows behind you."

"Wow is all I can say."

"Enough about me Mr....tell me about you. And you can start with your name."

He raised his glass and took another sip; a delaying tactic. He needed time to think.

"Emmanuel," he replied fictitiously.

In the world of preachers and pastors, it was more commonplace to lie, rather than be truthful; because they were held to a higher standard. Their image could be shattered overnight by a single piece of unverified information spread by word of mouth.

"Okay Emmanuel."

"You are here at a wedding alone. And there is no ring on your finger. I guess it's safe to assume you are not married."

"It's never safe to assume," he responded.

Gathered at the table in the rear were church goers Amber, Victoria, and Deacon Carter, who also observed Cole's presence and proximity with the woman.

"Well I must say I agree with you."

"And you should. No different than me assuming you were here on behalf of the bride or groom. Learn from my mistakes."

She struck him on the shoulder; a gentle blow; like a love tap.

"Are you getting smart with me Emmanuel?" she asked, tilting her head; arms crossed.

"Oh no, not at all," he answered, flashing his eyebrow; Ogling her for longer than a couple of seconds. She was like a prized possession being showcased in a maroon strapless dress; a one-piece outer garment that told a story; a narrative of erotic events; shiny; zipped in the back; cleavage partially exposed; hugging her hips like a mother's love.

She noticed his strong eye contact.

"Awe okay. I was just checking."

The reception advanced smoothly through the customary father-daughter dance, mother-son dance, and cake cutting. Cole and Karmen rambled on, gauging each other's interest. She was very affable, maintaining the flow of conversation; their social interaction was as if they had known each other for years. Good hearted kidding and teasing; occasional smiling; the kind of smiles that were misconstrued; the ones that started rumors; and it was only a matter of time before those newsworthy rumor mills ran at full speed around the ballroom.

"Hey Pastor how's it going!" the gentleman interjected.

Cole turned around. He had a neural disorder. Almost as nervous as the time he preached his very first sermon.

It was one of his associate ministers.

"Hey Minister Brennan how you doing man?"

Cole was hoping he didn't mention him by name.

"I'm doing good. Didn't mean to disturb you. Just wanted to acknowledge you that's all."

"Awe man, you know you not disturbing me."

"By the way this is Karmen. Karmen this is Minister Brennan" Cole said, establishing their acquaintance.

They shook hands; he looked at her with ambiguous eyes; as if he knew her more personally. But he dismissed it given the thousands of members at their church.

"Well Pastor, I'm getting ready to leave and go home. Just wanted to speak to you."

"Okay man you be careful" he said as they fist pumped.

The cake was now cut, and the Disc Jockey started back on the turntables, mixing up music for those wanting to trade in their slices for one last twirl on the dance floor. They tango and boogied; side step and two step, and after about a half dozen songs, just about everybody cluttered the floor; it was the electric slide; a song that always leaves lasting impressions.

"So I hear the beaches in Dominican Republic are almost as pretty as you" Cole stated, unnecessarily boosting her self-esteem.

Karmen blushed; refreshing smile.

"Awwww. Look at you" she said, pinching his cheek.

"Thank you, Emmanuel. That was very sweet of you."

"No problem."

"But yea I love the beaches in D-R. I try to go as often as I can. My favorite is Punta Cana."

"Punta Cana" Cole repeated.

"Yep. Punta Cana."

"And speaking of beaches," she said, leaning towards him, as if they were having a private discussion; she clinched her pinky nail between her teeth; slowly; amorous overtone.

"Would you like to have sex on the beach with me?"

He was appalled by the eargasm; inexpressible; un-anticipating her daring request. He was hesitant to respond.

After a few speechless seconds, "don't freeze up honey…sex on the beach," she naughtily expressed.

Running her finger along the rim of his glass, "Is my favorite drink."

Cole was tickled; drawing back his lips, as a soft laughed spilled from Karmen's throat.

Smiles of joy were replaced with concerned whispers amongst the guests at the reception regarding the aura between Cole and the estranged woman. They seemed to be a little bit too in-sync with one another, and there wasn't a plausible reason in their minds why he would be escorting Karmen out of the ballroom.

Sitting at the bar-line in the lobby, they sipped and savored; buzzing on drinks, while having what seemed to be a clandestine conversation. Karmen was very positive and upbeat, flaunting her alluring cute gestures, while communicating remarkable words to Cole. She was spilling out short stories, a handful of sexual innuendos; her indicator for determining how 'with-it' he really was. Her carnal needs sent her out for a one-night stand. After giving her both a personality and sexuality evaluation, Cole discerned that she was a risk taker and wasn't a politically correct type of person; she was addicted to thrills. And it was quite obvious to Cole that he was being propositioned for a rendezvous.

“Would the two of you like to have another round?” asked the bartender.

“Yes we would” Karmen responded.

Cole reached for his wallet.

“Oh honey I got you,” she said, as she pulled out a $20 bill from her purse.

“Okay. I have a question for you Emmanuel.”

“I have an answer...hopefully” Cole responded.

Twirling a strand of her hair, “what's six inches long, two inches wide, and drives women wild?”

He laughed away at her inquiry.

“There you go again,” he said, a reverence to her

bold overtures.

She smiled coyly; she was a super sexual, and wasn't into expressive symbols like roses and candy. She gave precedence to a simple bottle of wine or to fuck on hotel balconies.

"Ummm." he mumbled aloud, as he could discern Karmen was preparing him a platform for something exotic. It was a war between her will versus his morals. And the way Cole gazed at her she already knew that he lost the battle.

"Can you give me a hint?" he asked, pondering over her question, but at the same time, deciding on rather he would allow her to talk him into sleeping with her.

Breaking their contact barrier, she brushed her cheeks against his.

Just above a whisper, "you have it in your pants."

Cole simpered.

"Is that right?"

"Yep" she answered, fondling the pearls around her neck.

She hunched back in her bar stool.

Waving her $20 bill like an American flag, "moneeeeey."

The night was thriving as Karmen stayed on the same wavelength, broadcasting her intentions through her body language along with inadvertent touching. And Cole was philandering, as he knew he could have an encounter with her without future interactions; no strings attached. Karmen wasn't even a friend-of-a-friend-of-an-acquaintance. She lived out of the country, and was only in town for a few days, which made it even more compelling.

The coordinator ushered everyone to the outdoor steps so Alex and Hannah could make a grand exit from the reception, and be cheered off to a wonderful future. But unbeknownst to Cole, he was like a boy reading a comic book at the corner store, forgetting why his mother sent him there in the first place; to homage the nuptials. Cole was reckless, not even trying to avoid suspicion. He abandoned his self-conscious as he was caught up in the moment; unsuspecting that guests spotted him at the lobby bar with Karmen as they departed the ballroom. And under a modern conservative dictatorship where homosexuality and children out of wedlock were no longer frowned upon like old times, publicly cheating on your wife was too over the top.

Like lovely companions on the beach waterfront, they walked down the hallway of the 21st floor.

"What is it you need to show me? Cole asked gullibly, knowing Karmen was accompanying him to a forum of satisfaction.

No matter how hard he tried to stay in good graces with his savior, the heart still wants what it wants. And what Cole wanted was more than lust, it was a raw-essential need.

"Don't worry about it Emmanuel. Just come on," she said.

Entering into her 408 square foot suite decorated with warm colors, there was two Queen size plush beds, and contemporary furniture.

Karmen grabbed the Do-Not-Disturb sign and hung it on the exterior door-handle, shutting the door behind her, as Cole stood near the edge of the first bed visually scanning the room. He was in uncharted territories, driving a vehicle of sexual starvation and had a sweet tooth for human contact; but only desperate enough to pull up into a stranger's sleeping quarter for a quick drive-thru rather than dine-in.

Karmen removed her dangling diamond earrings and laid them on the desk as she passed by. She walked to the far end of the room, closing the long curtains draping over the floor-to-ceiling window.

Like a runway model, she spun around facing him with a sultry stare. Irresistible posture; his eyes wandered all over her; Cole plunging in the moment.

She removed her shiny dress; she had an Arizona tan; body glistening in her G-String and open tip bra. She finger-directive him to come, feeling empowered. Cole fell prey to her hip circumference.

He unloosed his David-Hart necktie and tossed it across the room. His suit coat followed. Then he slowly pursued; wondering if this was the right thing to do. Those thoughts quickly crumbled. Cole looped his arm around her. They began playing the kissing game; tonsil hockey. Swapping spit. Cole kissed her in ways that made her feel special; like she was the only woman in the world. She was a closet romantic, but openly true to her zodiac; Gemini. Curious and spontaneous; frequently solicits strip clubs and swinger parties on a whim.

Cole nuzzled on her neck with a hard on; her scent drifting into his nostrils. Karmen shivered. Everything about him stimulating her senses.

He pinned her against the high-altitude window; Vigorously. Her arms raised vertically above her head; their fingers entwined. Her heart thumping wildly. His pulse galloping. What was hard was now harder. The feeling of sin turned him on.

Minutes got lost in a blur of emotion, seduction and them shedding away their clothes. And what was harder was now upright; Cole had two years of pent-up sexual frustration aching for release; a release worth going to hell for.

Cole raised one of her pretty legs, cuffing it under his forearm. Her back against the window; he flexed his hips and slid halfway inside.

"Oh!" she moaned as she clung to him, trying to balance herself like a ballerina on one leg.

Cole withdrew and refilled her again.

Her face cringed, "Ewww...Emmanuel" she quivered.

He thrust; went in deeper. "Eww-Yes!" she moaned seductively; clawing for grip at his shoulder blade.

Her planted leg trembling; Cole elevated it. Both legs dangling over his forearms; spread apart. Back pinned onto the glass pane. She was now totally submissive. Her pleasure at his mercy. Her steamy desires heightened by his masculinity, manliness, musculature; his naked body clothed in strength.

He thrust harder. "Oh! Emmanuel!" he was fully inside.

He thrust; she clung to him. Her escalating melodic moans like poetry to his ears.

And again, he thrust. They met in rhythm; her dainty-voice groaning; body exploding into a thousand pleasing pieces.

Cole was in a meditative trance; thrusting; breathing erratically; sensual chemicals overflowing his cerebral arteries; her soft-wet geni like a massive dose of vitamins; curing his loneliness.

"Oh Emmanuel!" she screamed, leaving nail marks on his back; the marks of the sex beast.

He was thrusting in a recurring pattern; exerting pressure along her sensitive clit. Thrust for thrust. She was shuddering moans and lavish praises.

Her body was quivering. She was rushed with a sensation that started in her pelvic.

"Ahhh!...Ahhh!...Ahhh!...Oh yes!"

She began to shiver; the sensation spread to her curling toes.

"Uhhh!..Ahhh!" she moaned endlessly; involuntary vaginal contractions. The feeling was ethereal. Karmen was multi-orgasmic; she had an intense, unexpected out-of-body-orgasmic experience.

*****

A man will show his true colors by how he treats you after he cums. Karmen lied on the bed in a daze. Stupefied. Partially incoherent. She was still throbbing; aftershocks. Could feel him inside of her, but he wasn't there. Cole left immediately. Post-orgasm forehead kissing, affection and pillow talk aren't proper etiquette for one-night-stands; especially for a married man. Cole got what he wanted; meaningless sex. But so did Karmen. She wasn't necessarily craving reassurance and feeling neglected. Her needs were beyond met. More than she actually bargained for.

[Jenna...9:02 P.M.]~~**Hey baby where are you at?**

Jenna was lying in the bed.

[Cole...9:02 P.M.]~~**I'm almost home. I had to stop and get some gas.**

He was driving down the highway, with a boost of self-confidence; wearing an afterglow smile.

[Jenna...9:03 P.M.]~~**Okay I was just checking on you. I am getting ready to leave and go to the store.**

[Cole...9:03 P.M.]~~**Okay cool. I will see you when you get home.**

Over an hour later...

Waiting for Jenna to get home from the grocery store, Cole laid in the bed in his night clothes. Emblazoned on his mind was life, God, and the things that just transpired between him and Karmen at the wedding reception and hotel. His life wasn't a crystal stare. There was a murky maze in his ministry as he dealt with the divine and demonic simultaneously. Nevertheless, he was very grateful for the undeserving mercies that God had bestowed to him over the years.

Jenna made it home. After putting away the groceries, she came into their master bedroom, kicked off her shoes and snuggled up with Cole in the bed.

"Did you check over the power point slide show I emailed to you yet?" she asked, as she wrapped her arms around him.

Jenna was now his assistant. Naomi no longer assumed that position. She moved back to Atlanta after accepting a job at Spelman College as an administrative supervisor.

"No not yet. I will in a few. I'm kind of exhausted now from the wedding."

In a sarcastic tone, "Oh yea, by the way. How was the wedding...Emmanuel?

He couldn't resist a smile.

"It was amazing."

Curving the corners of her lips, "Oh really?" she asked amusingly.

"Yep."

They both laughed out loud.

"But did you see how Minister Brennan was looking at me when you introduced us?"

They mentally reflected on that moment...

("Hey Pastor how's it going!" The gentleman interjected.

Cole turned around. He had a neural disorder. Almost as nervous as the time he preached his very first sermon.

It was one of his associate ministers. "Hey Minister

Brennan how you doing man?"

Cole was hoping he didn't mention him by name.

"I'm doing good. Didn't mean to disturb you. Just wanted to acknowledge you that's all."

"Awe man, you know you not disturbing me."

"By the way this is Karmen. Karmen this is Minister Brennan." Cole said, establishing their acquaintance.

They shook hands; he looked at her with ambiguous eyes; as if he knew her more personally. But he dismissed it given the thousands of members at their church.)

"That was so close! He was looking at me like '*I know this woman from somewhere*.'"

Jenna disguised herself as Karmen, wearing a wig and makeup, with an imitative mole.

(He finally made eye contact with her. He was very perceptive. She had a distinctive tiny mole above her lips; like a young Cindy Crawford.)

By no surprise, considering she was an aspiring actress, Jenna longed to roleplay with her husband and immerse herself to spice up their marriage. And because she wasn't able to enjoy her original dream wedding by walking down the aisle, she was inclined to piggy-back off Alex and Hannah's ceremony and live out one of her unconventional sex fetishes themed '*Sexual Rendezvous with a Stranger*.' She always wanted know what it was like to be treated as a slut.

"Yea I was getting kind of nervous. Hoping no one

would find out" Cole said.

"But then again I knew they wouldn't. Everybody still thinks you are in Chicago. And nobody knows you are able to walk now."

It was a life changing moment. His prayers were answered several months ago. Cole was beyond excited when he saw Jenna stand up and take multiple steps on her own. Like a young man who just heard the NFL commissioner call his name at the NFL draft, he was overjoyed and gave God a play-by-play praise, thanking him for the supernatural healing of his wife.

"But they are going to know tomorrow morning though" Jenna said with a huge grin.

Jenna now had a different attitude, as she re-framed problems as opportunities for growth. She's spontaneous and lives more in the moment, and her love for Christ is much deeper than it was prior to her healing.

"Stop playing Cole!" a ticklish Jenna yelled as Cole was lightly stroking her hypersensitive areas. There was a sweet merriment amongst them. They engaged in a lovey-dovey wrestling match and gave each other kinky lip service before punctuating their night by making love.

Chapter FINALE

It was near the ten-o clock hour. A slew of believers dressed in their Sunday best rushed into the sanctuary of Abundant Faith. The majority of the fashion landscape were men sporting jackets and ties and women in their stylish skirts. However, the contemporary audience appeared to have gained in numbers. Forgetting that 'come as you are' is a matter of lifestyle and not attire, they had on baggy shorts, blue jeans and tennis shoes. And one lady in the rear slid into the pews carrying coffee in a plastic foam cup as if she was in Starbucks. Sister Mayberry, the usher with a kindred soul, whom everyone loved and respected, kindly asked her to discard it.

The excitement and energy was contagious. The praise leaders of brown and blue eyed soul singers rallied the congregants and set the mood as musical instruments enhanced the tone and beat. It was very enriching. But the highlight of the musicianship and worship experience was after the conclusion of Donald Lawrence's *'I am healed'* that they sang in unison. That song stirred up the spirit and magnified the ambiance. Hands were clapping; feet tapping. Their voices were exaggerated with *Hallelujahs* and *Thank-You-Jesus*. The keyboardist instigating the inevitable with lingering complex chords. And near the altar and between the pews, men and women shuffling their feet rhythmically;

the jingling disks sounded as the flamboyant tambourinist began to strike his hand against it. And when the organist strung together keys in up-tempo, there was a praise break, a cathartic release amongst the worshipers as their legs and feet shifted at a frenzied pace.

"I would like to invite your attention to the book of Second Corinthians, chapter twelve, verses seven through ten," Pastor Cole stated from the pulpit, wearing his purple and black clergy robe, laced with a cross on both sleeves.

There were over three thousand standing for the reading of the scripture. It was jammed packed; eclipsed capacity; the church body uncomfortably close. A portion of them had to sit in the overflow and watch the service on the screen projector.

He read aloud the passage.

"Now before you take your seat, I want to read verse nine again which is my focal point."

"And it reads... 'My grace is sufficient for thee. For my strength is made perfect in weakness.'"

"Thank you, you may be seated."

Everyone took their seats.

"Today I want to speak from the subject...Grace for grownups...Grace for grownups."

"Amen Pastor!" someone blurted out, as the media ministry displayed his subject and verse on the giant drop down screen hanging from the ceiling.

Pastor Cole opened his sermon with an interesting story; holding everyone's attention, including Cherokee, all the way back home in Santa Monica,

California, who chimed into the service online by logging onto the church website. Cole hadn't interacted with her via web cam in quite some time; he canceled his membership. And she was extremely curious to get an update on him to see if he was at least still alive and okay.

The meat of his message was beyond satisfactory.

"Sometimes, God will not change your painful circumstance. However, he will give you the grace to deal with it!"

"Preach!" someone yelled.

"But how can something as beautiful as the grace of God be so painful?... how can something so wonderful cause me to hurt?... can I illustrate it?"

"Go head Pastor. Take your time!"

He began to provide them an explanation.

"It is like a husband who wants to show his wife that he loves her...and so he buys for his wife a box of freshly cut roses...he gives her the box and immediately her eyes are beaming; her heart is palpitating. She is extremely ravished and excited about this box."

"Yes sir, Yes sir!" one of the deacons responded.

He continued in decorating a mental image.

"So she opens the box and she can smell the aroma...And instinctively she reaches her hand inside of the box and grabs the roses...but!... she grabs them by the stem."

Cole paused; scanning the audience.

"Immediately pain shoots up her arm!"

He was very demonstrative.

"Blood begins to blush out of her hand. She's bleeding profusely. Something so beautiful but yet something so painful...now she has a choice!... she can say to the rose...rose, I reject you...because you hurt me...you caused me pain."

The worshipers were intellectually tuned in; enamored by his practical application of the text.

"Or!... she can become angry with her husband and say '*joker if you really love me you would've taken the time to shave these thorns off the stem*'!'"

A choir member behind him clapped her hands in agreement. "Oh Jesus. My My My!" she expressed, as her spirit identified with his articulation.

"But you know what she does?" Pastor Cole asked rhetorically.

"Surprisingly, she doesn't throw the rose down. Nor does she become angry with her husband."

Giving them a visible description, he grabbed the flexible goose-neck microphone holder that was mounted to the podium.

"She continues to hold the rose by the stem!... in spite of the pain...because she knows!... that the intent of the giver was not to hurt her, but to show her how much he loved her!"

An abundance of shouts and screams permeated the sanctuary.

"Come here let me ask you a question."

He hand-signaled to them.

"Can you hold God by the stem!"

"Yes! Yes! Yes!" the people of faith yelled, as they stood up from their seats.

"By the stem when a loved one dies!... by the stem when the doctor says it's cancer!..by the stem when you laid off from your job!"

Pastor Cole began to preach them to a place abstract preaching couldn't quite penetrate; similar to Rod Parsley; a Caucasian adopting expressions of a black preacher.

His linguistic patterns became rapid, "This type of Grace is not for little boys, or little girls...this is Grace for Grown-Ups."

His verbiage was soulful, and rhythm inviting. A soundtrack of whoops that they ceremoniously heard every Sunday; a celebratory style of closing with melodic chants, where responses were exuberant, validating their connectedness with his engaging sermon; sanctioning their kinship of the same faith.

The service was exhilarating. The glorious fellowship proved to be a meaningful experience. Souls were saved, lives were changed; people departed the sanctuary feeling refreshed. They heard a soul stirring message, but also witnessed the miraculous wonders of God through a strange but encouraging change of events. During the call to Christian discipleship, a woman walked down the aisle from the back pew, and stood at the altar alongside the other guests who were joining or seeking baptism. It was Karmen, that same woman whom several of them saw at last night's wedding reception with Pastor Cole. But when she removed her wig and dark glasses, they instantly realized she was their First-Lady; the one they seen restricted to a wheelchair in recent years is now standing independently. They were astonished. Spines tingling, hairs on the back of their necks raised. Their prayers and petitions were answered. Many fell to their knees in worship.

Just over two months later...

"Have a seat sir." Cole expressed to the mailman that just entered into his office.

He drooped down on the loveseat across from the desk, where Cole was sitting.

Cole was on the phone; feeling euphoric; yakety-yaking with Jenna.

A minute or so elapsed.

"Alright baby, I'm going to let you go. I have a client that just walked in."

"Okay. Well I guess I will see you tonight at 7:30 when you get there" Jenna said.

"Actually, I am going to get there *very early* for you. I will be there at 6:30. In the front row."

Her fancy became reality. She was chosen to perform in the hit play *THE MOTOWN MUSICAL,* written by Berry Gordy, at the Repertory Theatre in Nashville, TN. She was a lead character in the production.

"You better be."

"No doubt."

"I love you."

"I love you too baby...and good luck tonight."

"Okay talk to you later" Jenna said.

Cole ended the call.

"Sorry about that."

"Oh no problem" he responded.

"Soooo...how's work treating you...Is it hot enough out there for you?"

"It ain't too bad. I've had much hotter days than this."

"I hear ya...well I don't want to keep calling you mailman, so if I am not mistaken your name is..."

Cole glanced down at his printed document.

"Mr. Jake Burns."

"Yes that's me."

"Okay Jake thanks for coming. But before we get started, may I get you a bottle of water or anything?"

He removed the postal cap from his head.

"No, I am okay."

"Are you sure?" he asked genially.

"Oh yea, I am good. I keep plenty of fluids with me in the LLV."

"LLV??" Cole repeated in a questioning tone.

"My mail truck. LLV is the technical acronym for it."

"Okay. And what does that stand for?"

"Long life vehicle."

"Oh really. Wow I never knew that...that's interesting."

"Alright then...with that being said, tell me what seems to be the problem?" Cole asked.

Jake placed both hands on his knees.

"Well, I actually have three problems."

He was in his early forties; Caucasian; dark brown hair, with a receding hairline.

"Ok. Well just tell me exactly what those problems are."

He let out a dramatic sigh.

"Well...my first problem is..."

He paused momentarily; mentally getting his thoughts together.

He exhaled a deep breath; appearing flustered.

"My first problem is...I'm in love with a bitch I can't stand."

Cole raised his eyebrow.

"Ohhh-kay," Cole responded. He was somewhat surprised by his abrasiveness, even though he didn't mind it.

Cole affirmatively nodded his head for Jake to continue.

"My second problem is...I'm in love with two women."

Jake had a serious disposition.

"Okay...and, your third problem?" Cole asked, as he rested his elbows on the desk with his fingers interlocked.

"My third problem is that...one of those two women that I am in love with...is the bitch that I can't stand."

Cole closed his mouth, pushing his tongue against his teeth; stifling a laugh and a smile. He knew this was going to be an interesting session.

Read on for an excerpt from

TROIS: *Monogam-ish Marriage*

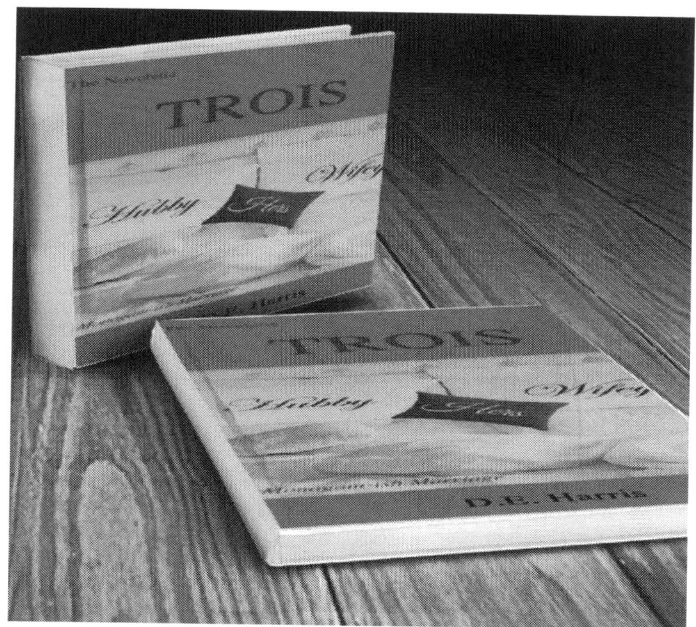

The E-Book

Casually browsing the newsfeed on her facebook page, she noticed red icons suddenly lingering over both silhouettes.

Who is Ginger Fowler? **an inquisitive Kate thought to herself.**

She momentarily disregarded the friend request, as she began to read her messages.

Ginger Fowler____*"Hello Miss Burke how's life in sin city treating you today?"*

Kate Burke____*"Oh I can't complain. What about yourself?" she replied.*

Ginger Fowler____*"Honey I am doing just fine, but I will be much better when I finally arrive in Vegas soon"*

Kate Burke____*"Cool. What brings you here?"*

Ginger Fowler____*"You...LOL...LBVS"*

Ginger Fowler____*"I'm bi -curious but extremely particular about my encounters. That being said, I believe you are absolutely suitable for my standards."*

She was very candid and didn't diminish her intentions.

Given her novel approach and appearance, Kate immediately accepted her request to become friends.

A Columbian descent, Ginger's father was Spanish

and her mom was black. She was well proportioned with shapely legs and pleasing curves. And even though Kate's emotions gave precedence with only men, her sexual appetite was unrestricted.

Leisurely scrolling through Ginger's pictorial, she was strikingly impressive, and delighted Kate's visual senses.

"*What the hell...Oh my goodness,*" Kate softly uttered. Her attention escaped to the smiling man who was hugging Ginger.

That's the same exact guy from Houston that messaged me last week **she mentally reflected.**

She had a puzzled look on her face.

A week prior, he solicited Kate's inbox expressing his desire to get more acquainted with her, which comprised of shopping and fine dining. Although he was tall, lean and muscular, fairly handsome, and extended a generous offer, he was beneath her interest at the time.

Kate Burke____ "Who is the guy in all these pictures with you?"

Ginger Fowler____ "Oh that's my husband. He's the gentleman that reached out to you not long ago...I encouraged him to."

Kate Burke____ "What was the purpose

behind him contacting me?"

Ginger Fowler____ "The same exact reason I want to get in touch with you. We would love for you to accompany us on our vacation out there in Vegas...But let me explain.... A little over a year ago, I cheated on my husband with another woman. I was always very curious and finally acted on my desires without his initial consent. But after it happened, I was straightforward with him, and from that point, we agreed that I could have sex with another woman, but never apart. He would have to be present. So over the past several months, my husband and I have experienced swinging a few times. He's getting comfortable with it and so am I. So I told him about you after coming across your profile and bio. Your pics and presumed persona was very appealing to me. When I showed my husband your profile, you tickled his fancy very strongly as well. So I told him to email you first with the proposition. But obviously, you were not very receptive so that's why I am on here contacting you."

Kate Burke____ "Well I'm certain your husband is a wonderful gentleman, but I wasn't too fond of interacting with him on that level. I get approached very often by men, and sometimes it gets old. Plus, I wasn't too sure of the validity in his offer."

Ginger Fowler____ "Trust me, I understand exactly where you are coming from."

Over the next several months, they exchanged pleasantries via Facebook. Primarily shooting the breeze but occasionally naughty thoughts. There was a heightening shared excitement as their discussions became more intimate, and it wasn't long before they felt at ease with one another.

GINGER Fowler____ "Hello Kate hun. How are you? I must admit I am a little bit concerned about you. It's been quite some time since we have chatted. I hope I did not offend you or say anything out of bounds. I know sometimes my blunt remarks and honesty can be volatile to some......"

There was a brief discourse between Kate and Ginger, and she became mildly anxious about her welfare; mainly because Kate had yet to respond to any of her previous messages. But unbeknownst to Ginger, life and business matters became overwhelming for Kate; she strayed from social networking sites for a couple of weeks.

Four Days Later

Kate Burke____ "Hey hun. I am just now getting your messages. And to answer your question, no you have not said anything displeasing to me. In fact, I love our conversations on here. I just decided to get myself in order because I was getting behind on personal issues. But now I am back in the swing of things. So don't worry. I am doing just fine. By the way, how have you been?"

Ginger Fowler____ "Hey I am doing great! Girl I am relieved to know you are okay and that I didn't do anything wrong to you. That being said Kate, give me your number if you don't mind, that way I can have another way of contacting you just in case you or I are not online."

Kate Burke____ "Ok but my number right now is for ONLY YOU...Can I trust you to keep it confidential?

Ginger Fowler____ "For sure hun...Pinky Promise."

Kate Burke____ 702-243-8369

Ginger Fowler____ "Excluding your area code, I like how your number begins with TWO and ends with SIXTY-NINE. LOL

For successive days to follow, the rekindled companionship began to blossom. After sharing erotic slideshow photos and illicit text messages, their amorous desires for each other was mutually at its peak.

Wearing a megawatt grin, "Welcome! How may I

help you all today?" the front desk clerk asked.

"We have a reservation for Dave Fowler" he responded. Adjacent to him was Ginger drooping in her posture. She was exhausted from the flight delay and long layover.

"Ok Mr. Fowler, may I please see your license and credit card" the clerk requested.

Their ears were fond of the game bells and ringing slot machines permeating the atmosphere in the Wynn hotel lobby.

Antsy to meet each other, they finally established a common resolve where Kate would spend time with them in Vegas. She was comfortable with an arrangement of pairing on all social affairs, but when and if sex came into play, Dave could not participate. Ginger, a trust fund baby and owner of a dance studio favorably regarded by the general public, was financially adequate and reassured to Kate that she would be well compensated for her time.

"Here are two keys for you. You will be in suite number 1257. Walk down that hallway and you should see the elevators on your left."

The pinnacle of exclusivity, their vision of luxury changed upon seeing unexpected art paintings sporadically hanging from the crystal-encrusted wall textures around

the room. As they stepped onto the dark hardwood floors, they couldn't help to notice soaring tall ceilings, with high altitude windows in the rear, where guest was afforded true sophistication amidst breathtaking views of the Las Vegas skyline. Inspired by rich shades of chestnut and ex

presso, the immaculate penthouse suite was infused with fashionable contemporary furniture, featuring ebony countertops in the kitchenette, and in each bathroom marble tiles creating a feeling of splendor. They were certain to enjoy their stay as they expected to take full advantage of the wet bar, Jacuzzi, and advanced technology it provided.

Buzzing with joy “Kaaaaate !!” Ginger expressed with open arms. They embraced each other very tightly.

“Hey! Good seeing you! How was your flight?” Kate asked. Showing her likeness for fashion, she was wearing a light orange skirt; brief in length, a sheer peach summer blouse, complemented with tan stilettos.

“Uhhhh. I wasn't very satisfied at all, but at least I made it.”

“Well I am glad you all arrived here safely.” Kate said as she quickly glimpsed over at Dave.

“Oh my goodness forgive me for being so rude!” Ginger uttered in a self-conscious tone.

“This is my husband Dave” Ginger said, extending

her arm in his direction.

They engaged their torsos affectionately, as Kate and Dave officially acknowledged one another. He was dressed business casual; brown slacks, with a fitted light blue Ralph Lauren collared shirt, and the scent of his Burberry fragrance was satisfying.

There was an exhilarating aura as the trio was amused to be in each other's proximity. As promised to Kate, they had just spent several hours buying commodities from stores and cutting edge boutiques filled with high fashion, designer labels, and signature bags.

Retrieving an American Express Card from Dave, "Is there anything else I can get for you all today?" asked the server.

"Ummm" Dave uttered, as they all made contact with each other.

"No ma'am I believe we are just fine."

"Okay well I will return momentarily with your receipt." said the waitress, before heading back towards the kitchen.

It was a starlit evening as they found themselves dining at one of Vegas' premier steak houses, gulping down elegant spirits and eating overpriced salads.

“So Kate how old is your daughter? Ginger asked.

“She is twenty.”

“Really!” Ginger responded. She was mildly astonished.

“Yep. Not kidding. She is a junior in college at UNLV. She's studying kinesiology.”

Ginger took it upon herself to rest her hand on Kate’s thigh.

“Honey. You don't look a day over twenty-five, so for you to have a daughter in college is...”

Struggling to find a word, Ginger was a bit tipsy. And so was Kate; slightly intoxicated by wine.

“Izzzzzzz...fucking amazing” Ginger uttered sluggishly.

From dawn to darkness, it was an adventurous evening as they were en route back to the Wynn hotel, cruising in the white Range Rover they rented. Although Kate and Ginger dominated the majority of all the dialogue, the vibe was still harmonious, as Dave was relishing the presence of two beautiful women.

“What floor are you going to?” the blonde haired-blue-eyed tourist asked, standing next to the wall plate.

“Floor twelve please.” Dave responded.

Light illuminated from push buttons 12&4 as the service elevator ascended. Unreserved in their conduct, Kate and Ginger stood intimately close, as they were not ashamed to behave amorously.

Only a few moments elapsed before the trio exited the elevator upon hearing the bell sound.

Passing the threshold of the suite, "Hey Dave, where is your restroom?" Kate asked.

"Oh it's right there to your left" he said, pointing in that direction.

He went to the bedroom cornered in the back end of the penthouse to change into more comfortable attire.

Ginger, wearing her form figured short dress and *Jimmy Choo* heels, gently tapped the privacy control button on the remote, shutting the curtains to the high-altitude windows.

A long hard minute surpassed when the door to the restroom opened as Kate was leaning over the sink cleansing her hands. Instinctively, she glanced up into mirror and realized it was Ginger; beaming, craving licentiously for Kate. It was apparent by her mischievous grin.

Twisting the faucet knob clockwise, Kate suspended the water flow. She turned around, facing Ginger; cheeks flushed. She couldn't resist her pleasing smile.

Ginger seized her by the hips, pulling her closely. They affectionately saluted each other with their lips. It was a thrilling kiss. Kate's hormones burst into full throttle.

She cuffed Ginger's bottom like a soft melon. With both hands. Elevated her onto the his-her sink.

Kate's palm traced her inner thigh. Sinuously. Slowly towards her erogenous area. Ginger's heartbeat rapidly increased.

She vehemently gasped as she touched Ginger's smooth Brazilian geni.

Ginger sighed a gratifying sigh as she was being tantalized. The peak of Kate's tongue exploring creases of her glistening geni lips.

Warm breath and saliva. Her clitoris swelled. Kate sucked until it couldn't grow any further. It was enormous. Throbbing and pulsating.

She went in slowly with her speech organ. And told a freaky-tale. Ginger whimpered. Her geni was dripping wet.

"Ewwww-Shit!!....Ahhhh!" her whimpers escalated to tumultuous cries of passion.

Ginger grabbed Kate's hair. A fist full. She pulled her into greater depths, aggressively rubbing her geni against Kate's face; her lips were coating Kate's lips with her fluid.

Ginger's voice peaked "Ohhh!! Ohhh...Shiiit!...O God!..Oh, oh. Ewwww—Shit!"

Kate lifted one arm as she collider her tongue with Ginger's clitoris. She seized her around the neck. Ginger was cringing. Pinned up against the mirror at the shoulder blades; drowning in moanful cries in Kate's chokehold. Manhandling Ginger. She savored it. And the fact that it was a woman only magnified the feeling.

"Ohhhh....ahhh, ahhh, ahhh!!" Ginger outcried in short recurring intervals. She had a sense of constriction in her chest, as her breathing was difficult and noisy; like a respiratory disorder. Her body had surrendered to the tortuous rhythm of Kate's tongue.

Unexpectedly, they gained the site of Dave as he was standing at the door. He was bare back, and exposed, only wearing dark gray Calvin Klein undergarments. In one hand he was holding a bottle of wine, with the other he was groping his disc.

Ginger began managing all sensations of her new pleasure with closed eyes; Pre-cum face, nearness of her orgasm. Her insides quivering, knees collapsed onto Kate's shoulders. She could barely breathe. Her face buried in Ginger's geni. She never came up for oxygen.

Ginger climaxed. Cum smudges on the side of Kate's chin. She was turned on by it. Wondering if men felt the same way when she went down on them.

Dave, with his eyes fixated on the twosome, had

surpassed his normal mode of concentration. He was broker. A damn good one. Accustomed to reviewing the Dow Jones and habitually studying recent trends on the New York Stock Exchange.

Loud moans escaped from Ginger. Her back arched. She squirted. Creamy sauce. Gratefully shouting, in ecstasy, as if she was worshipping her sex God.

After a quartet of orgasms, Kate pulled away from Ginger's breathless body. Ginger satisfied, but wanting more.

"Make sure you take plenty of pics of us" said Kate, as she handed Dave her I-Phone.

He unveiled a lopsided smirk.

Naked and unashamed, they all became one with nature as they settled on the outside balcony. Dave was still clinging to the same bottle, and Kate brought out an additional bottle to share with Ginger.

There was a twofold splash as Dave and Kate dipped into the hot tub followed by Ginger cradling her legs across Kate's thighs facing her.

Kate wasted no time before she started fondling on Ginger's perky breasts. She was enamored of them.

She ushered Ginger to come closer; She obliged.

Exhaling a passionate sigh, Ginger reclined her

head displaying contentment with Kate nibbling on both her hard nipples in unison.

Dave, from the opposite end of the jacuzzi, had begun snapping photos at Kate's request.

In a seductive tone, "Ewwwww" Ginger emitted, as her D cup tits were drawn into Kate's mouth. She was tingling with pleasure.

She reciprocated the favor and began caressing Kate's breasts; thoughtlessly.

Like a skater on ice, Ginger proceeded to glide her expert tongue over Kate's receptive nipples. They were incredibly horny, indulging in each other's delicacies. Kate loved sucking titties and Ginger loved having them sucked.

Kate navigated her hand like a submarine.

"Ahhhh" Ginger freakishly moaned, as Kate was finger-loving her below the bubbly water.

Their body temperatures were increasing; partially perpetuated from wet steam, but mostly sexual tension.

While gulping champagne from the bottle, Ginger slowly gyrated her geni on Kate's fingers. Dave was recording the sexcapade with Ginger's cellular; audio and video. Spatter of swift water currents with all their movements. He was wearing a privileged smile. The display of their lewdness through the camera phone more enticing than his guilty pleasure; adult films. Pornhub was now a distant second. But if it featured *Julie Cash* **then it**

was a close second.

Kate commissioned Ginger out of the Jacuzzi as she laid her head back over the border of the whirlpool. Ginger's body dripping wet, she crouched; ass all over Kate's face, moist opening brushing onto her thick lips.

"Ohhh yes" Ginger said, as Kate's tongue was causing friction against her sensitive clit. She was mesmerized by how amazing her lips and tongue felt inside of her and it wasn't long before she started trembling.

"Ohhhh!!" she moaned seductively. Her sweet nectar flowed into Kate's mouth and down her chin. Dave spectating. Just an arm's length away in the hot tub. Jacking-off; like a voyeur of women sexually enjoying themselves.

Kate tumbled Ginger over onto her back, positioned her knees on each side of her head and sunk down to her face.

"Ahhhh" She shuddered erotically as Ginger licked on her swollen spot. She had a aquafina flow.

Kate maneuvered her geni around Ginger's tongue, steering her to desired areas.

She was a fast learner.

Kate let out indefinite moans...legs tensing...thighs shaking...a discharge of her intoxicating juices smothered Ginger's lips.

It was long overdue. His participation came to fruition as they went to the cabana, located on the lower deck of the balcony.

Dave hurled Ginger on the bed; face down ass elevated.

"Ewwww Shiiit!" Ginger uttered as he shoved his sex muscle in from the rear. He was heavily equipped.

Dave parted her geni with deep hard thrusts; enraged with sexual energy.

"Ooooooh yeaaa! fuck me daddy!"

And that he did. He took masterly control; pounding her geni ferociously. Imposing his will on her.

"Ohhhh yes! Fuck me harder, harder!" she commissioned.

Laboring husky breaths, he stroked relentlessly; stared ahead into Kate's eyes. She was on the opposite end of the bed. Dave hoping she would trade places. But the polyamorist sat quietly; intrigued by the novelty fuck session.

"Yes! Fuck this pussy daddy!"

Ginger had a dominating personality, and was sexually dominant, but cherished being fucked in submissive positions. Particularly doggystyle.

"Oh yes! Fuck me real good daddy!" Ginger screamed, raking her nails across the satin sheets.

Dave was showing no mercy. Fucking the shit out of her. Supremely, with an animalistic expression.

"Oh yes! Un hn, Yes! Yes! Fuck me!" Ginger uttered. Her geni was aching with pleasure.

Like he was auditioning for a role on Broadway, Dave was trying to impress Kate, gazing straight ahead at her. Grimacing, growling, aggressively driving his hips towards Ginger's curvaceous-jello ass.

He glanced down at his waist line; White secretions smearing onto his big disc, violently pumping her drenched-cum geni.

He pulled out; abruptly; lightly tapping his disc on her ass cheek.

"Ahhhh!" he exploded, as warm heat was surging throughout his body.

"Ahhh...Ahhhh!" followed another eruption of fluids. It was a considerable amount, partially covering the body art on her lower back.

In a baritone pitch "Uhhh" he muffled, slowly dribbling his remains onto her.

Dave busted nuts all over her ass in courses.

Ginger was drained, Dave was exhausted. They expended all their energy into the evening of passion.

Physically depleted, the threesome snuggled closely on the cabana bed like a baby in dreamless slumber.

Kate, couldn't have asked for more. The weekend concluded with more shopping and dining. For her time spent, she was compensated enough money to pay two mont hs mortgage and a car payment. But unbeknownst to her, this was only the beginning.

Standing at the curb, Kate waved her hand to get Ginger's attention.

"Hey girlie!

"Hey hun! It's good to see you!" a smiling Kate said after opening the door on the passenger's side.

"Where you want me to put my suit case?" Kate asked. It was a Dolce and Gabbana with a black leopard canvas that Ginger purchased for her during the shopping spree in Vegas.

"Oh girl just throw it in the back seat. It is not a big deal."

Pulling away from the George Bush terminal, they immediately began wagging their tongues as they were overflowing with good spirits.

"So how are things going for you at the dance studio?" Kate asked Ginger.

"Oh it's going pretty good. I am actually going to stop by there on the way home and let you take a look at it."

"How is your daughter doing?"

"She's doing wonderful. Still in school making good grades, and got her a boyfriend now."

"Uh oh" Ginger expressed sarcastically.

"Exactly. That's how I felt, especially since she didn't offer to share it with me. She normally tells me about all her flings but I had to find out about this one through casual conversation."

"So how did you find out about him?" Ginger asked.

"One Saturday afternoon we were sitting around the house bored, and I asked her if she wanted to go see *Fifty Shades Darker* **with me and she told me she had already seen it with Jeremy...I'm like, who is Jeremy...then she told me he is her boyfriend."**

"Oh wow"

"Yea but even though she never told me about him, I do trust her choice in guys she dates. They are normally well mannered and respectful."

"That's good. Have you met him?" asked Ginger.

"No. But I am soon. My schedule has been cluttered,

and she is also busy. So we have never gotten around to it. Plus they are still new. Hell by the time I return back to Vegas, they may be broken up by then. You know how these young kids are.

"Yea that is definitely the truth."

Traveling at a moderate speed on highway 59 headed south in Ginger's pearl white Mercedes Benz S 500, they were listening to *979 The Box Houston*, **moderated by** *Jillian "JJ" Simmons*, **one of the nation's most vibrant on air personalities. It was hot and sunny and both Ginger and Kate dressed accordingly. Ginger, with her hair pulled back in a bun, couldn't help but to command a lot of attention, as she was wearing her skinny jeans and a short sleeve V neck where her full breasts were partially uncovered. Kate was sizzling in her own sexiness as she was sporting a khaki skirt at mid-level length, a purple summer top complemented with Valentino heels and designer sunglasses by Jimmy Choo.**

Noticing the distinct building "What is Whataburger?" Kate asked inquisitively.

"Girl, that's a fast food restaurant where they sell these huge hamburgers. I am not a big fan of them though...But don't let me discourage you from trying it out. Never know you may like it."

"Oh I won't" a smiling Kate responded.

About a half hour passed before they pulled up in

the parking lot at Ginger's dance studio located in River Oaks.

Together they strolled into the building.

“Hey Ms Ginger,” she said, as the sound of the bells on the door handle lingered. She was leaning against the desk, looking like a trophy wife. The kind that Kate would love to fuck.

“Hey how's everything going today?”

“It’s running smoothly. But a customer called and wanted to know what days and time we would be offering salsa dancing classes this fall. He wanted to register for him and his wife.”

“So what did you tell him?”

“I didn't tell him anything. I just took his number and told him I would get back with him by the end of the day.”

“Ok great. Just call him back and let him know that it will probably be on Tuesdays and Thursdays at 7, and Saturday afternoons. But we will know for sure by end of next week.”

“Ok.”

“But hey Christine this is my friend Kate, Kate this is Christine. She's my executive assistant.”

They greeted one another with a gentle handshake.

Christine was pale skinned with long honey blonde hair flowing down her back, wearing a white T-Shirt that traced her softball breasts.

Ginger proceeded to show Kate around the facility as they tarried and mingled with other staff and a few guests. They were very hospitable.

"And last but not least, this is where I transact most of my business" said Ginger, smiling amiably. She closed the door behind her and locked it.

Kate was in awe upon entering the office as she had such an appreciation for good taste.

She sailed around slowly, attentive to the features. It was uniquely characterized. Aside from a large creamy desk with photo of Ginger and Dave arranged next to the computer, there was a silver metallic waterfall mirror straight ahead on the wall, a purple futon stationed horizontally in the corner, and custom made curtains.

"Oh my! This is very nice." said Kate, giving special consideration to the abstract oil painting.

"Who made this?" she asked curiously, lightly striking her fingertips on its canvas.

"Umm. Her name is Marie. She's African decent; an art professor at Rice University."

Kate read aloud the label beneath it.

'The Moment Of Intercourse'...2009."

She couldn't help to simper as she glanced over at Ginger. She was a few feet away, biting her lower lip, heavily gazing at Kate, wearing an I'm-going-to-fuck-you face.

Kate and Ginger had matching lust for each other, but in a different way. For Ginger, Kate was like her lover, her dream girl, but for Kate, Ginger was her whore.

Kate took a second stare back at the artwork as Ginger stood directly behind her, fiddling her fingers through her hair.

It was an invited distraction.

Brushing away the strands, she roamed her exotic tongue around Kate's grateful ear.

Her pulse quickened. "Ahhh" said her tender-dainty voice, as she expelled a large quantity of air. It was a pleasing sigh.

Ginger's whispered into her ear; an indecent command.

Kate rendered to her will; bent over the desk; exhibiting her fatty bottom.

Ginger raised Kate's skirt. Bundled over the back; just above her tramp stamp. She was turned on by her soft ass, thick hips and enormous thighs. And Kate was already steamy and ruttish. Ever since she hopped on the plane, she was jittery and antsy. Could barely remain seated throughout the flight.

Ginger swatted her ass and massaged it gently.

She slid her index finger into Kate's geni. She shuddered with pleasure. Her middle finger followed, she shuddered with greater pleasure.

They could never suppress their desires while in the presence of one another as almost every scenario became exotic.

After a sizzling series of finger strokes, Ginger sampled her own fingers; tasting Kate's sex.

"Lay up on the desk" Ginger said.

Abandoning the promise she made with her husband, she was poised to fulfill her fantasy of having Kate exclusively.

Kate surrendered; lying on her back on top of the desk, spreading her legs like a butterfly.

Ginger flickered on her clit with her tongue. Just outside of the door, the staff working and the guest rehearsing dance routines.

"Aaaahhh!" she moaned, as her body exploded into thousands of pleasing pieces. Sex sounds inaudible; drowned out by the music blasting from the ceiling and floor speakers.

Her back arched "Ohhhh!" she groaned. Ginger was licking and sucking her clitty-cock in all the right places; intensely. Kate fondling her own aureolas. She had nipple rings. They didn't want to draw attention to

themselves, but they were more turned on by the possibility of being noticed.

Kate's legs began shivering; she curled her toes; her body movements were variant; the pen container fell onto the ground.

A few heartbeats elapsed. Kate busted cum-loads onto Ginger's face.

Ginger wiped the cream from around her mouth and didn't say a word. With a pure conscious, she exited the office calmly; casually. Just as she would after a board meeting. And Kate laid motionless, feeling larger than life.

"Well hello lovely ladies" Dave stated as Ginger and Kate passed through the door leading to their garage.

"Hey baby. We are finally here!"

"Well it's good to see the both of you. I was getting a little worried there for a minute. I didn't know if yall were okay or just having a bunch of fun without me."

Ginger pinched him on the cheek, "Oh no worries honey bunny…I took her to go see the studio and we just hung out there for several hours."

"Oh ok cool."

"Hey Kate it's good to see you again."

"Likewise" she responded, looking up into his dark brown eyes. Fairly handsome, he had a chiseled physique and stood 6'2". He was well groomed with a freshly cut low-fade pompadour and goatee.

"Come on and follow me. Let me show you around the house" said Dave, retrieving the luggage from her grasp.

In the heart of Lake Olympia subdivision was their five bedroom waterfront home, nestled amongst the gated community of Flamingo Island. In the kitchen was a gourmet island with granite counters, stainless monogram appliances including a double convection oven, and wine cooler. In the master suite was a fireplace and adjoining study, large bay windows with views of the lake, motorboat, pool, and lush landscaping of the backyard waterfall and firepit. Perfect for entertaining, there was a spacious game room with a wet bar, and state of the art media room, as well as a covered balcony.

"And finally this is the room where you will be at."

Adjacent to the gameroom, the spacious guest suite was graced with a King size bed, a 46' high definition flat screen TV on the wall, and a black dresser drawer with attached mirror.

"You can just put it up here on the bed" said Kate.

Dave placed her luggage on top of the bed at her request.

"Ok. Well make yourself comfortable. Mi Casa Your Casa. We will be downstairs hanging out if you desire to join us."

"Yea ill come down there in a minute after I get myself situated."

"Ok Cool" said Dave as he left the room.

Over a glass of wine, Kate very briefly socialized with Ginger and Dave around the kitchen bar as they expressed their opinions about the latest scoop on the television show 'The Bachelor.' Immediately after her last gulp, she vacated to the upstairs guest room and quickly fell asleep. She was completely exhausted.

Lounging on the sectional, she was reading a novel during commercial breaks but her general interest was on the flat screen television as she was watching her favorite talk show *The View.*

"Well good afternoon Kate" said Dave as he walked in the front room. He drooped down on the far end of the couch.

"Hey Dave buddy. I thought you would never wake up."

"What you mean...Girl I been up since seven this morning."

"Really?"

"Yea! Around 8:30 or so I cracked the door to the guest room where you were sleeping to see if you wanted to go to Cracker Barrel for breakfast but you were knocked out. Sleeping good. So I just left you alone because I didn't want to disturb you."

"Man. I was so tired"

"Yea I could tell"

There was a brief moment of silence.

"So what book is that you reading?" he asked.

"Uhhh. It's titled THIS IS KNOT WHAT I PRAYED FOR"

"This is not what I prayed for" Dave repeated.

"That's an interesting title."

"Yea it is. It caught my attention when I was at Barnes and Noble the other day to pick up something to read while on the plane...It's a really good book...I give it a four out of five star."

"Oh really. That's cool...So who's the author?"

"D-E-Harris"

"Oh really! Okay...I love D-E-Harris' writing style.

I've read Harris' other books and columns."

"So Kate, I was thinking."

"About" she stated.

"I was thinking about the bond that you and Ginger share. I could tell you two had an instant connection and a sweet vibe...And that same exact energy you all have is what I would ultimately like for all three of us to have together with each other. I know that you are not as free with me as you are with Ginger which is cool and very much understandable. But in order for us to all have that same vibe, you and I will need to develop a good connection between us separately from Ginger…

Dave drooped down on the couch next to her.

"So basically, my point is, I would like for you to consider spending time with me on a one on one basis so we can get more comfortable with each other. And if you are okay with it, I will definitely compensate you substantially for your days with me. Before you know it, your house would be paid off completely...So what do you say?"

Kate quickly pondered. And in her subconscious, she **knew it would be beneficial to capitalize on his offer. With a daughter in college, she was now money driven and had hopes to start up her own concierge company in the near future.**

"Actually Dave, I do kind of see your point...Why don't you let me think about it and get back with you on it

ok...I need to re-evaluate my schedule and daily routine and see if I can squeeze you in...I just don't want to make any promises I can't keep."

"Ok that's fair. I completely understand. Just think about it and let me know what you come up with."

Accentuating the shape of her eyes, she was staring into the bathroom mirror as she applied a dark tint to her eyelids.

Suddenly, she was interrupted by the ringing of her I-phone.

"Hey Ginger honey how are you?" Kate said upon answering her phone.

"I'm good babe! What are you up to?"

"Oh. Not much. Just getting ready to head to the movies with my daughter. She finally made time for me." Kate said, anxiously glancing around for Dave.

It was the following month after her initial visit when Ginger had to go out of town on business. Kate agreed to Dave's proposal, as he sent for her to fly into Houston while Ginger was away.

"Oh ok that's cool...Hey I got a quick question for you"

"What's up?" Kate softly responded. She was feeling uneasy. She didn't want Dave to have knowledge of their conversation, but at the same time she wanted to hide her truth from Ginger of being in her home with Dave.

"I was wondering if you can fly into Atlanta in the morning to accompany me while I'm here. If so, I'll go ahead and book your flight tonight."

"Oh honey I won't be able to make it for another couple of days. I have a lot going on here in Vegas that I need to get squared away. How about Monday afternoon...Is that feasible?"

"Yea babe that's fine. Monday afternoon it is. I'll book it within the next hour and email you the itinerary."

"Ok cool."

"Well enjoy your movie with the mini me!"

"Ok I will."

Kate hung up the phone feeling relieved. She proceeded in applying cosmetics to her face as she was preparing for an outing with Dave.

Earlier in the day, he asked Kate what they could do to make her feel more at ease around him. She mentioned her aspirations for strip clubs, as she was unpretentious in the presence of sexy women. But unbeknownst to Dave, Kate was actually content with him. It was just that her conscious was constrained by the notion of sleeping with a married man, even though she

had sex with his wife Ginger, a married woman. Nevertheless, playing "uncomfortable" was her perfect counterbalance she planned to drag out for a lengthy time. It enabled her to delay sex with Dave but yet receive satisfactory payments.

"Ohhh" a startled Dave said, as he walked out of his bedroom fully dressed. He unexpectedly saw Kate sitting on the sofa.

"I was just getting ready to come upstairs to check on you, but I see you are already dressed to go."

"So how long you been waiting?" he asked.

"I've only been down here for about five minutes, if that...But hey, I just got an emergency call while I was in the bathroom. I am going to need to leave here on Sunday night to get back to Vegas."

Given that Ginger was steering the illicit affair, satisfying her desires were more prominent than Dave's and she was compelled to speak untruthfully.

"Sooo, is everything okay with you?" Dave asked in a sentimental tone. He had an unpleasant feeling within.

"Oh yea no worries. Everything is just fine. I just have some family matters to address."

"Ok that's good to know. I feel a little better now."

"So you think you will be able to make it back

before Ginger returns from Atlanta?"

"I'm not sure, but if I can I will definitely let you know."

"Ok cool. Just keep me up to date…So you ready to roll?"

"I am as ready as I'm going to be!"

"Alrighty then, lets head out."

Throughout the night, they didn't have much to say while at Club Dream, Houston's most premier gentleman's club. They nursed on crown and cokes, and a bulk of their time was spent upstairs, where guest were afforded private dances. *Chastity Red,* was specifically chosen by Kate. At face value, her dimensions appeared to be adequate, somewhere around 36-27-45. She had smooth skin with a peanut butter complexion, full lips, and conspicuous dimples when smiling. But what stood out the most was the distinctiveness in her voice. She had a Cuban accent.

Dave reveled in his viewing pleasures as Kate and Chastity Red were the main attraction. He was buzzing; Nodding his head to the hardcore lyrics of hip hop artists; witnessing their lascivious acts. After a myriad of songs and several rounds of Tequila, Chastity Red was being finger seduced by Kate as she rhythmically gyrated her ass

on her lap. She was groaning, erotically, while Kate sweet talked her, but her groans were overwhelmed by the loud music. Dave, was snared in the moment by Kate's seductive ways, and she noticed his prolonged gaze. It was undeniably evident. Similar to the stare when he watched her fuck Ginger in the bathroom at Vegas' Wynn Hotel.

After a couple of hours of steamy stripteases, the club was closing down for the night. *Chastity Red* was the recipient of over $600, afforded by Dave.

From the very first exotic lap dance, a unique aura evolved between Kate and the stripper. She told Kate that she was from Milwaukee and that her name was Amber when they exchanged contacts. And Kate made no secret of her intentions when telling Amber her plans to frequent Houston in the coming weeks and months.

"Damn, I'm kind of hungry" Dave stated, after shutting the driver side door of his BMW 750Li

"Yea me too." Kate responded.

"I knew I shouldn't have been drinking on an empty stomach."

Dave was tipsy and slightly nauseated.

"So what do you want to eat?" he asked.

A particular fast food restaurant came to mind that Ginger told her about on her last visit.

"I want try that Whataburger place...Is that cool?"

"Sure! Let's hit up Whataburger. You will like it I'm sure." Dave said.

They pulled out of the parking lot en route to satisfy their appetites.

It was normal routine. Kate maintained monthly visiting relations with both Ginger and Dave as well as individual arrangements between them on separate occasions. She enjoyed a threefold compensation as she capitalized on the couple's deceptive ways. Ginger wasn't aware of Dave meetings with Kate, and Dave was oblivious of his wife's affairs with her. Although she continued to decline Dave's desire for sexual intercourse, she granted other favors whenever she saw him. As his payments increased, the more she permitted. When they left club Dream, she jacked him off in the car on their way to Whataburger. A week or so later, his wild fancies heightened to where he was privileged to toy his dick between her butt cheeks, masturbate over her ass and cum on it. And not much longer after that, she let him eat her out geni and likewise, she sucked his dick like she invented it. Dave was so in lust with Kate, but never did she allow him to engage in vaginal sex with her.

8 months later

A single parent with a daughter in college, and a first-year business owner, Kate was now relying on Ginger and Dave to maintain the comfortable livelihood she managed with the support of her ex-husband. She was no longer governing her thoughts and actions by moral principles, but she was now saying and doing anything, as her services for Ginger and Dave took priority over all matters.

"Hello" said Kate as she answered her phone.

"Hey Kate!" She seemed to be very ecstatic.

"Hey Ginger what's going on? You seem to be in great spirits this afternoon."

"Because I am!"

"My studio is growing and I am very optimistic that I will be able to plant a location in Vegas within the next year."

"Cool!...Congratulations. I'm happy and excited for you." Kate responded.

"I actually have a conference there tomorrow evening and will be flying in tonight to celebrate. And what

better person to paint the town red with than you."

"Awww really…That's cool. You know I'm down."

"So what about Dave? Is he coming as well?" Kate asked.

There was a long hard pause. Ginger didn't say a word.

"Why? Do you want him to join us?" Ginger finally answered.

"Not necessarily. I was just asking. It's whatever makes you comfortable and happy. After all, it's your celebration."

Kate and Ginger practiced all aspects of lesbianism, exploring the aches and joys of anal sex with strap-ons. Never before did Ginger have anal sex with Dave, although he always longed for the reality with her. The ladies experimented with fruit penetration and also had a threesome with another woman Ginger knew, and as time progressed Ginger became emotionally attached to Kate. She would purposely set up business meetings in other cities outside of Houston just to get away from Dave as he could no longer satisfy her affectionate needs. She was yearning for an open permanent relationship with a woman; particularly Kate. Although Kate was a bit uncertain of what Ginger specifically wanted, she was intuitively aware that whatever it was, it didn't involve Dave.

Ginger quickly changed the subject, "So where

would you prefer to dine? I'm going to call and make reservations for this evening?"

"It's a Japanese restaurant called the Yellowtail in the Bellagio. I think that will be pretty suitable for the toast."

"Ok hun. Well I am going to call them and reserve us a table. I'm on my way to the airport now and will text you once my flight land."

Damn. How did I let my selfish ways break up a happy marriage she deeply reflected as she hung up the phone.

Seemingly, Ginger was falling for Kate and she was disturbed by her blended thoughts. Because she never had an arousing interest in Ginger emotionally, the sexual affair was complicated as her attraction for Ginger was only physical.

Had I just agreed to let Dave get involved in the beginning, maybe none of this would not be happening.

Kate began to feel guilty deep down inside as she felt partly responsible for how Ginger was betraying her husband and wanted to leave him. She sided more with Dave realizing he was not only totally in love with Ginger, but the sole reason he agreed to the threesome was to satisfy and please her.

She continued to speculate...*How do I fix this? Maybe I will just cut them both completely off that way they can focus on their marriage together...Or what if I told her I don't want a relationship with her beyond sex and money? Would she be okay with that? But damn, I am a struggling business owner and the money is too good to right now to risk her not being okay with it.*

Given Ginger's manipulative nature, Kate was antsy to resolve matters quickly before the triad became more complex.

Just a few hours from an X-rated freak session in the hotel room, Kate, Ginger, and Dave sunk their bottoms into a comfy sofa at the Bellagio, and intimate bar and lounge. Nearby, was a roaring fireplace as the cozy atmosphere was enlivened by live music of the band. Enjoying a traditional Japanese cuisine dish along with endless rounds of wine, Ginger and Kate fell into a conversational rut, whispering into each other's ears their fanciful erotic filled imaginations of what they are going to do to each other once they returned to the room. Dave, at the far end of the couch, was in a zone, nodding his head as he gave a full hearing to the music, but periodically

chuckling to their filthy discussion he overheard. As the night advanced, they drank more and more. And the more alcohol Ginger and Kate consumed, the more contemptuous language they uttered to one another.

"Come on honey I'm tired of sitting down, let's get up and dance." Ginger commissioned Kate.

Ginger's mood was cohesive with the music and wine. They joined other patrons on the center floor to express their pleasures by artistic motions, moving nimbly. They were under Dave's observant attention as he remained seated, gently swaying to the tempo of the beat. It wasn't long before they behaved savagely while dancing. As she stepped rhythmically, Ginger grazed her bra-less breasts against Kate's.

There was an instant hot stream flow running down her inner thigh.

Let me get off this dance floor before we end up in a puddle **Kate thought to herself as she tightly clamped her thighs together. She was panty-less and wearing a short dress.**

Ginger continued dancing sultry, as she slowly rubbed Kate's hips and ass.

With warm cream streaming between her thighs, Kate subconsciously carried onward an excuse to take a seat. She was feeling a bit uncomfortable and wanted to escape from potential embarrassment.

Yea they need to spend time together anyways and rekindle some things

She composed a sequence of dance steps towards Dave, grabbed his hand and escorted him over to Ginger.

After sitting back down on the couch...*Damn that was a close one. This bitch turns me on, I can't deny that* **she thought to herself.**

As the band played, Dave and Ginger moved about merrily, taking measured steps. He wasn't ashamed to serve Ginger's provocative appetite, firmly grasping her ass while they maneuvered accordingly with the music. Ginger was inflamed with joy; stimulated in the moment.

Suddenly, when the sound of the instruments ceased, so did Ginger's high spirit. She was agitated.

Exhibiting her displeasure, Ginger gave Dave a long hard stare before making a rapid flash away from him.

"Come on Kate let's go!" an angry Ginger said as she grabbed her Louis Vitton bag. She was woozy, walking unsteadily.

Dave rushed over to furnish her with stability; lend a hand. She was staggering and it was very apparent.

She pushed him away. "Come on Kate, I want to go!..Fuck!"

Kate was baffled; had scattered thoughts.

"Without his lying, cheating ass!" Ginger said, as she faced towards Dave.

"And get your own fucking room because you won't be sleeping with me tonight!"

Ginger was enraged.

Both Dave and Kate was in a state of mental numbness. They glanced at each other wearing dazed expressions, before staring back at Ginger with ambiguous eyes.

"Ginger. What's going on"? Dave asked in a confused tone.

"Those drinks got you tripping. Do you hear yourself right now"?

Although Kate wasn't showing anxiety, she had a nervous tension.

Damn how did she find out? Did someone see us together? Now my money is down the drain and I don't have a backup plan.

Kate's mind was racing.

"Yea muthafucka I hear myself! And I am not that damn drunk to know you been hanging out at strip clubs, taking bitches to dinner and paying for hotel rooms! You are a piece of shit for a man!...Yea you dickhead I saw the receipts in your pockets at home...Did you really have to go fuck a stripper behind my back? Really Dave!...After we

agreed to do everything together!"

Dave was on an emotional roller coaster, feeling relieved but perplexed.

Ginger continued in her tirade...

"A stripper in our city Dave!..huh!...Fuck you Dave! Go back and get your stripper bitch and spend our money on her! Trick it off on a sleeze bucket with diseases!"

Ginger was an elitist, and stereotyped adult dancers with sexually transmitted infections.

As they paced through the hallway of the lounge to exit "Oh…And I didn't see a receipt for condoms you nasty muthafucka!" Ginger was irate.

"I didn't fuck her. All I did was get lap dances and we went to breakfast, got a room and talked...nothing more." Dave said, attempting to trivialize her presumptions.

Kate was holding Ginger by the arm for support as they walked down the sidewalk to the Taxi Lane. She felt at ease by Ginger's misconception of Dave cheating with a stripper and not actually her.

"Ginger! I'm sorry baby. I just needed someone to talk to." Dave said apologetically. He was standing just a few feet away from her.

When the cab pulled up next to them at the curb, Ginger quickly swung open the door.

"Don't wait for me in Houston because I will not be back at the house!..I will be finding myself another place!"

After Kate got in, she sat down in the back seat of the cab and slammed the door.

Standing by the door with her luggage..."Kate honey I've been doing a lot of soul searching lately and I find myself thinking of us being together in a greater capacity." Ginger said, as she could no longer restrain her true feelings.

Kate remained stationary, quietly listening, with no intentions to contribute to the conversation.

"I really care for you a lot baby and I'm certain you probably feel the same way about me. So when I get back to Houston I will be going to rent out a condo and I want you to stay there with me more often. I really need your presence and support at this time in my life given everything I am going through right now."

Kate continued to give Ginger her undivided attention, as she took the envelope into her possession. It was full of money.

"And as you know, I will more than likely be opening a studio here soon so we will definitely be able to spend more time together even while we are here in Vegas."

Although Kate was nodding her head in agreement, she was discombobulated.

"But anyway babe, I gotta go before I miss my plane."

Ginger and Dave were still feuding, and made separate travel plans to get back home.

"Ok be careful. Text me when you land." Kate responded.

"I will baby. By the way, I'll be booking you a flight out to Houston next week once I get settled."

"Alrighty."

Ginger leaned towards Kate and kissed her intimately, but it was unpleasant to her nature. Kate was instantly sickened by it. Ginger kissed her as if she was kissing her husband she was in love with, and for Kate that was disgusting.

Tightly embracing her "Ooooh baby, I miss you already." said Ginger.

"I miss you too" Kate responded very dryly, lacking feelings.

A gloomy Ginger headed downstairs and rode on the hotel shuttle bus to the airport terminal.

713-487-3928 **were the numbers Kate dialed from**

her iPhone immediately after she left the room.

After only one single ring "Hello...Hello" Dave answered with a tone of urgency. He was waiting desperately for Kate to call him.

He utters her name, "Kate"

"Hey what's up. Are you ok...Have you tried calling Ginger?"

"I've been trying to call her all morning, but I never got an answer...And I was going to call you but I didn't want to piss her off even more and make matters worse...Where is she at? When did you see her last?"

Actually, she just left here a few minutes ago."

Well did she say anything else about what happened last night?...and where did she say she was going?" Dave asked. He was very concerned about his wife's state of mind.

Kate's conscious was tugging her to inform Dave of Ginger's intentions, but she couldn't suffice herself to tell him.

"She just told me that she was headed out of town for the next several days...That's really about it. We didn't talk at all about what happened last night or anything like that."

Given the abrupt turn in their marriage, Kate couldn't help but to reflect on her livelihood and personal

business. Although she was living comfortably off of the money Ginger and Dave was paying her, the love triangle she found herself in was becoming a bit stressful. The constant traveling and going back and forth between the two of them was mentally and physically straining. She felt helpless, like a puppet on a string, she had no control over her own life. Nevertheless, she continued to attend to their needs as she felt it was her best option right now.

The week following....

"This is the room where you can unpack and hang up your clothes, but you will be sleeping with me in the master." said Ginger, as she was delighted to have Kate as her live-in girlfriend.

It was a spacious two-bedroom plush condo with security-gated entrance, located in Katy's far west side.

Shortly after Ginger walked out, Kate organized her shoes and designer bags, and began hanging up her clothes in a systematic arrangement. It was a walk-in closet that extended far and wide.

Several long moments surpassed before Ginger re-entered the room, lustfully gazing at Kate as she stood at the threshold of the closet. Kate's back was facing her as

she didn't't' notice Ginger's presence. She was in a zone, coordinating her belongings in such a way that appeases her.

She turned around to grab another hanger. Her heart fluttered. She wore a startled expression as her eyes found Ginger standing directly in front of her.

With energetic pursuit, Ginger backed her against the dresser drawer and invited her hand under Kate's shirt.

Kate allowed her to remove it. And piece by piece, she undressed her. She unhooked her bra and watched it fall off her breasts. She took off her shorts followed by her pink thong.

Grounding onto her knees, Ginger passed her agile tongue over her index and middle fingers, enticingly, staring up at Kate. She was aroused by Ginger's tempting invitation, knowing it was only a matter of a few minutes before she was going be tongue fucked.

Her soft throbbing geni accommodated Ginger's fingers, massaging her slowly in provocative circles... Kate's pleasure juices rushing down Ginger's wrist, stream stoppage at the diamond bracelet she was wearing.

Her lips grips Kate's entire geni, warm breath stimulating her clitoris. Her legs weakening.

She sucks gently; it was brief...

Thanks for reading…That's All For Now

Brand Awareness Per D E Harris' Personal Likeness/Interest/Sponsorships

Kamica Hampton, (pg 2) Founder of Kamica Hampton Collection.

Instagram: KAMICAHAMPTON

Website: KHAMPTON.COM

SoloNoir, Chicago, Illinois (pg 51), Founded by Andrea Polk.

Instagram: SOLONOIRFORMEN

Website: WWW.SOLONOIRFORMEN.COM

GABEBABETV (YouTube) (pg 95), Founded by Gabrielle Flowers.

Instagram: GABEFLOWERS

Longs Bakery (pg 84). 2300 W. 16th Street. Indianapolis, Indiana 46222.

Cretia Cakes (pg 159), 4261 Lafayette Rd. Indianapolis, Indiana.

Instagram: CRETIACAKES

Website: CRETIACAKES.COM

Mecai Adeola, (pg 157) L'oreal-Mizani Artist. Studio, City California. Internationally Available:

Nigeria/Dubai/London

Instagram: 1MECAIMHX

The Breakfast Klub. (pg 30) 3711 Travis Street, Houston, Texas 77002

Marcus Cosby, (pg 49,150) Pastor of Wheeler Ave Baptist Church. 3826 Wheeler Ave, Houston, Texas 77004.

Stacy Spencer, (pg 48) Pastor of New Directions Church. 6120 Winchester Rd. Memphis, TN 38115.

Dexie Berries *(pg 73)* Indianapolis, Indiana

Instagram: DEXIEBERRIES

Jason Crabb (pg 83) National Recording Gospel Artist.

Instagram: JASONCRABBMUSIC

Website: JASONCRABB.COM

Maroon 5 (pg 148) Grammy Award winning pop-rock band

Instagram: MAROON5

Website: MAROON5.COM

Je'Melody (pg 128) Musical Artist, Charlotte, North Carolina

Instagram: JEMELODY

Single 'Addicted' Now available on iTunes/SoundCloud

Reco Chapple (pg 98) International Fashion Designer

Instagram: HOUSEOFCHAPPLE

Website: HOUSEOFCHAPPLE.COM

Kelli Evans (Actress/Public Figure) (pg132)

(YouTube: MissKellisWorld)

Instagram: MISSKELLISWORLD